The Fabergé Heist

(Matt Drake #21)

By

David Leadbeater

Other Books by David Leadbeater:

The Matt Drake Series
A constantly evolving, action-packed romp based in the escapist action-adventure genre:

The Bones of Odin (Matt Drake #1)
The Blood King Conspiracy (Matt Drake #2)
The Gates of Hell (Matt Drake 3)
The Tomb of the Gods (Matt Drake #4)
Brothers in Arms (Matt Drake #5)
The Swords of Babylon (Matt Drake #6)
Blood Vengeance (Matt Drake #7)
Last Man Standing (Matt Drake #8)
The Plagues of Pandora (Matt Drake #9)
The Lost Kingdom (Matt Drake #10)
The Ghost Ships of Arizona (Matt Drake #11)
The Last Bazaar (Matt Drake #12)
The Edge of Armageddon (Matt Drake #13)
The Treasures of Saint Germain (Matt Drake #14)
Inca Kings (Matt Drake #15)
The Four Corners of the Earth (Matt Drake #16)
The Seven Seals of Egypt (Matt Drake #17)
Weapons of the Gods (Matt Drake #18)
The Blood King Legacy (Matt Drake #19)
Devil's Island (Matt Drake #20)

The Alicia Myles Series
Aztec Gold (Alicia Myles #1)
Crusader's Gold (Alicia Myles #2)
Caribbean Gold (Alicia Myles #3)
Chasing Gold (Alecia Myles #4)

The Torsten Dahl Thriller Series
Stand Your Ground (Dahl Thriller #1)

The Relic Hunters Series
The Relic Hunters (Relic Hunters #1)
The Atlantis Cipher (Relic Hunters #2)

The Rogue Series
Rogue (Book One)

The Disavowed Series:
The Razor's Edge (Disavowed #1)
In Harm's Way (Disavowed #2)
Threat Level: Red (Disavowed #3)

The Chosen Few Series
Chosen (The Chosen Trilogy #1)
Guardians (The Chosen Tribology #2)

Short Stories
Walking with Ghosts (A short story)
A Whispering of Ghosts (A short story)

All genuine comments are very welcome at:

davidleadbeater2011@hotmail.co.uk

Twitter: @dleadbeater2011

Visit David's website for the latest news and information:
davidleadbeater.com

Copyright © 2019 by David Leadbeater
ISBN:9781091665392

All rights reserved. No part of this publication may be reproduced, distributed, or transmitted in any form or by any means, including photocopying, recording, or other electronic or mechanical methods, without the prior written permission of the publisher/author except in the case of brief quotations embodied in critical reviews and certain other non-commercial uses permitted by copyright law. All characters in this book are fictitious, and any resemblance to actual persons living or dead is purely coincidental.

Thriller, adventure, action, mystery, suspense, archaeological, military, historical, assassination, terrorism, assassin, spy

The Fabergé Heist

THE FABERGÉ HEIST

CHAPTER ONE
PRESENT DAY

Jax was one-fifth of the greatest heist team the world had ever known. More than that, he was its leader. In its lifetime, the team had pulled off eight highly lucrative heists, each one so seamless, so brilliant, that their team had become thought of as ghosts. Many believed they were an urban legend, but even so they had been given a name: The One Percenters, because they were in the top one percent of all criminals around the world.

This was the start of their ninth heist.

Jax concentrated on keeping his profile as low as possible. Cara, Steele and Kushner were close by. They were all part of the entourage surrounding a large man with a great deal of bluster. Faye was staying remote as she always did—their tech geek, she handled everything from afar and was as distant during a job as she was when they were all together.

Jax looked around. They were inside an advanced tech lab in the heart of California, here to steal an item that would simplify their upcoming heist. Of his three companions, Cara was situated closest, her mid-length blond hair hidden under a black wig, steel-framed glasses concealing her model-like face even further, a high collar and padded clothing adding to the disguise. Both Steele and Kushner were similarly concealed. Steele was large anyway—he was the blunt instrument, the muscle of the group—which made Jax think maybe he'd gone overboard with the added layers. But maybe not. Nobody appeared to have noticed him.

Which was probably due to the brash, noisy Texan in whose shadow they walked. His name was Kirkwood and he was a billionaire looking to invest in the tech lab. Faye had spent weeks finding the right patsy—a man that courted and loved the limelight—and then getting Jax and the others added to his visiting entourage, complete with backstory and security passes. It hadn't been an easy task, and Jax had thought they wouldn't make it in time—the Las Vegas heist was planned for three days' time—on several occasions. He'd thought more than once that they would be forced to carry out the heist without the gripper gloves. But then Faye found this Texan tool they could use to cover their entry, and it was all go.

Jax watched everything. The lobby they walked across had a high domed ceiling, constructed of white panels and glass. Sunlight streamed through the windows, giving the place a warm, airy feel. Their footsteps echoed from the tiled floor to the ceiling, and there were many footsteps. Kirkwood came with a large support staff.

As a group, they approached a reception desk with Kirkwood's constant chatter claiming all the attention. The receptionist was already on the phone to inform of the important man's arrival and, in just a few seconds, doors at the back of the room opened and several suited men walked out.

"Mr. Kirkwood," one could be heard saying. "Thank you for coming today. My name is Steinfeld. Would you come this way?" There was a pause and then an added clarification: "All of you."

Jax fixed his eyes on the floor. The team knew where they were going and what they had to do. Faye had taught them the schematics of this place two dozen times. They knew where every camera was placed and how to avert their faces from the prying lenses. Or, at least, they thought they did.

When one of the automatic doors jammed, the man called Steinfeld let out a long sigh. "Apologies, sir," he said. "The computer system has been faulty for the last few days. I thought it was fixed." The look on his face told Jax someone would pay later.

The door soon reverted to normal, performing as it was supposed to. The system glitches were all part of the plan, designed to accustom the staff to them over a few days so that the one that allowed Jax's team to act would be considered just another malfunction.

Once in the lab's inner sanctum, Kirkwood and his staff were led along a curving corridor with windows to the left that overlooked landscaped grounds. To the right stood secure laboratories, most with their windows opaquely glazed. Jax knew it was done manually, at the touch of a button, and wondered what Steinfeld didn't want them to see.

They were nearing the moment when they would have to act. Cara, Steele and Kushner drifted nearer to Jax, faces taut but determined. Kirkwood pushed through a door into a large conference room. Jax checked their rear. Nobody followed.

Faye was in their ears, speaking over their secure comms. "Five . . . four . . . three . . ."

Jax readied himself. The lights flickered. An alarm rang and then stopped. Kirkwood shouted. Automatic doors and windows went crazy. Jax used the distraction to slip through a door to the left that led to a new wing, Cara, Steele and Kushner at his back. The CCTV system would be running on a temporary loop down this corridor. They needed four minutes.

Jax counted three doors, stopping outside one that read: *Advanced Anti-Slip Development*. He tried the door, working on the law of averages. Often, they were left unlocked and saved the team time. This one wasn't.

Cara was at his side. "You feeling good?"

He knew what she meant. "Save it for later."

Steele was at Jax's other side. The big man looked ready and mean enough to chew through the door if he was told to. Then Kushner pushed past.

"Make way."

Kushner was the consummate thief of the group, the pure artist. He was their expert and directed all matters concerning entry, exit and the robbery itself. Now, he spent seconds attaching a homemade circuit board to the door's keypad and finding its combination. The lock clicked open and they were inside. Jax moved to the front again, ready to give the orders.

"Far right." He pointed. "Grab the gloves. Make sure you get the display models and not the prototype." Kushner moved off. "Far left, liaise with Overwatch on the computers. Scramble everything to cover our retreat." Cara hurried over to a computer terminal. "And you—" he turned to Steele "—watch the door."

Jax stayed central, overseeing it all. Faye counted down the time. Three minutes passed. Kushner had accessed the gloves but had stopped moving.

"There's a second layer of security," he said. "Shit."

They hadn't anticipated that. Jax waited for Faye's next comment. "You have forty-five seconds."

"How good is it?" Cara asked, looking up, but still typing. "I'm about ready here."

"Not hard, but it's gonna take more than forty-five seconds."

Jax shook his head. "Not good enough. Cara, help him."

Kushner looked up, stroking back several stands of hair. "There's nothing she can offer that I don't already know."

Cara ran over to Jax. "I don't know what you love more. Your reflection or your brain."

Jax agreed but stayed quiet, gauging the situation. Forty-five seconds passed.

Faye spoke over the comms: "Ready to scramble their systems one more time in five . . . four . . ."

"Hold up," Jax said. "We have an issue here."

"The risk increases—"

"I know how the risk increases," Jax interrupted, feeling annoyed at everyone. They were flawless. They were practiced and well-informed. Only the best thieves carried out eight major heists without leaving one salient clue beyond a few grainy photographs. His anger rose, reddening his neck and cheeks.

Cara noticed. "Relax. Just relax. We don't want attention."

She was right. He fought it. Jax had always been shrewd, able to read and react to a situation almost instantly. But he was also ex-military and tended to treat threat with violence. For years now, he'd been able to rein it in, but lately had felt the vicious tendencies overpowering him. Cara said it would split their team apart. That, or get them caught. But then Cara was only here for the art, skill and ingenious fluidity of it all. She abhorred violence, which was why she hated Steele.

Lately though, Jax had agreed with their team's muscle. He'd hurt two bystanders and a guard this last month. Two of those attacks hadn't been necessary. One had been way over the top. Cara saw it all and pulled away from him as a leader. She was right. His changing attitudes could end the team, one way or another.

But Jax had good reason for his growing anger. He couldn't share it with the team. In fact, the last thing he could do was share it with the team. Jax had a secret—something nobody else on the planet knew, not even the so-called One Percenters that made up his legendary crew.

The secret was called Bella.

She was his wife, and he'd married her in total secret three years ago during a One Percenter hiatus. When the idea for the new Vegas heist had been floated by Kushner just three months ago, Jax had first checked with Bella. She'd had no problem with it. She knew everything about his past and the people he worked with. She knew and accepted that the heists, although dangerous, were what kept Jax and the others sharp, dynamic, on the edge of life and death, which was how they lived their lives best. Jax agreed and Kushner started a preliminary analysis of the heist. Cara and Faye helped.

Three days ago, when they were almost due to start, Bella disappeared. Jax went crazy, ransacking every local establishment for her. He'd even considered contacting the police.

But then he was contacted by a man who worked for a Mexican cartel. They had taken Bella and were offering to return her in exchange for both the fruits of their upcoming heist and his team. Jax had been stunned. Left speechless. As far as he knew they'd never crossed another criminal, let alone one as dangerous as the cartel. Kushner had been very particular about it in the past. They'd even anonymously paid two sets of thieves off on previous occasions, not wanting to step on their toes. Questions bombarded him. How had they known about Bella, about the marriage, and about the heist? How had they known where to find him and why did they want his entire team?

It seemed somebody believed the urban legend rumors weren't rumors at all and had been keeping tabs on them. And whoever it was wanted the Fabergé eggs.

Jax wished he'd never heard of the eggs. The upcoming heist had taken on a dark, desperate aspect. Jax reverted from a shrewd leader, able to calculate, watch over and pull together a job from gestation to completion, to the violent, ex-army man Cara had first met twelve years ago. Back then, he was a man trying to change and she'd helped him achieve that. Now, he was a man trapped in an agony of conscience, of respect for his colleagues, and love for his wife. The training was trying to take over.

Cara saw his struggle and questioned it. But he couldn't tell her the truth. He had to figure out a way to complete the heist, save his wife, and hand over the eggs without losing his entire team to the cartel.

"Done," Kushner interrupted his thoughts, holding the gloves in the air. "I have two pairs."

Perfect.

Jax felt a rush of relief. For a moment there it had felt like everything was falling apart before they even got going. He couldn't think that way. Bella's life depended on it.

Cara was eyeing him. "You okay?"

"Stop asking. I said I was good."

Steele backed away from the door, eyes angry. "Two guards coming."

"Here?" Cara asked, exasperated.

"Didn't wait to find out. I'll handle it."

"No." Cara stepped toward him. "Not your way."

"Don't worry." Steele flapped her away.

"Are you gonna harm them?"

"Well, I'm not gonna lick them."

Jax saw the team's infrastructure fraying. Things had

always been edgy between Cara and Steele, but it had been a minor issue. Well, that and Kushner's narcissism. Seeing the chance of a major problem developing, he stepped forward.

"You two relax. I'll handle this."

In his ears, Faye said, "I can always get them called away."

Jax was by the door, watching it open. Silently, he cursed Faye for not stepping in sooner. But she'd always been insulated from real life, a girl alone and apart, and had no feel for danger. He couldn't blame her.

"Hey guys," he said, stepping into the first guard's eye line. "You got that system fixed yet?"

"On with it. Where's your ID?"

Jax was furnished only with the visitor pass they'd gained by entering with the Texan loudmouth. They hadn't had time to steal and then create a genuine ID with the big heist going down in just three days.

"On the table," Jax said. "Let me get it for you."

He turned, letting the door close in the guard's face and beckoning Steele to get into position. The big man grinned, sliding behind the frame. Cara looked dismayed and ran forward, catching the frame.

"Hey," she said. "I'm sorry. He's too proud and too stupid to tell you he left his in the break room. Here, check mine."

Jax had been ready to lure them in and attack, but now fought down the urge. Cara wasn't taking too much of a chance. The break room was only four doors down and she'd lifted an ID from the computer desk she'd been working on. He admired her ingenuity. He knew she was trying to save the guards some damage, but doubted it was going to work.

"Says here your name is Jack Cross."

"Jac," she said. "Short for Jacquelyn. Someone made a mistake."

It was desperate. There were times when it might work. Guards that might accept it, especially when Cara smiled at them. But not with these two. They were dedicated to their work.

"Step back," one said. "We're coming through."

Cara stepped aside, shaking her head and looking down. She knew what was about to happen. Jax grabbed the arm of the first man to appear and wrenched him inside. The man staggered forward into a desk, the top part of his head striking a metal lip. Blood sprayed across the desk and down the side. Jax jumped on him. Steele took the second guard, stepping around the frame and punching him in the nose. The man fell to one knee, struggling to pull a Taser from his belt. Steele grinned at Cara for effect and then allowed the man to draw it.

"Bad move," he growled.

The guard's nose was bleeding. He wiped his eyes. Steele used that time to grab his wrist and bend it until the Taser was nestled against the guard's own chest.

Steele grinned into his eyes. "Told you."

He thumbed the switch. The Taser's charge made the man crumple. Steele kept it on until Cara pulled him away.

Jax took hold of the first guard's head and smashed it once more against the edge of the desk. He let go and the man struggled to rise. Jax punched into his kidneys and then his throat, sending him down to the floor, gasping for breath.

"That's enough." Cara had hold of Steele and raised a palm at Jax.

Jax landed on his opponent's back, knees-first, grinding

them into his spine. He raised a clenched fist, preparing to smash it into the back of the guy's neck.

"If you hurt him any more, I'm out."

Cara's words scared Jax. They couldn't pull this job off without her. And that put Bella in danger. He looked over, trying to force down mixed feelings of anger and fear.

"Don't say that."

"Then let's go. Now."

Jax pushed himself off the guard. Kushner was alongside them, holding the gloves. Steele checked the corridor and gave them the all clear.

Jax held Cara's eyes. "He'll be fine."

"We're normally the perfect crew. Legends. Ghosts. But something's going on. You're unravelling. Me—I love the thrill and the artistry of the heist. What are you here for now?"

Now? He caught the nuance in her question. He couldn't answer. He was reclaiming the merciless weapon mantle he used to have because he knew that, after the heist, he was going to need every advantage. Kushner moved off and Jax followed him, leaving Cara to bring up the rear.

Jax let them sort the exfil with Faye's help. He heard alarms and saw more shenanigans but didn't take much in.

Was Bella alive? How could he give his lifelong teammates to the cartel? Had somebody ratted them out?

The One Percenters were the best of the best, but there was no way they would survive what was coming.

CHAPTER TWO
THE LAST SIX MONTHS

Matt Drake sat in idle contemplation. It wasn't a state of mind he was accustomed to. It wasn't a state of mind he enjoyed.

A floor to ceiling window offered up a spectacular view. A short walk away, a gently rolling deep-blue sea lapped at a meandering bay and white sands. The window was about fifty feet above the ground, at the top of a cliff and part of a luxurious Caribbean hotel. Drake was sitting on the edge of a bed, naked, with a sumptuous gray duvet covering the important parts. He was relaxed. Not prepared for battle in any way.

It didn't feel right.

But it had felt much worse five months ago when President Coburn had agreed to create a new kind of rolling strike team that responded only to the gravest threats to the United States and its closest allies. Threats so great, it seemed, they never materialized.

A figure crossed his vision, walking past the window to the French doors. It was Alicia Myles and she captured every ounce of his attention.

"Ey up," he said. "Where've you been?"

"Breakfast," she said, stepping through the open doors.

He saw she was carrying a tray filled with two mugs of steaming coffee, croissants and butter. Not a bad way to start the day, but not as good as seeing her lithe, bikini-clad figure barely covered by a flimsy beach wrap.

"Dessert looks good," he said.

"Hold your horses, boy," she said. "Before you call her

dessert you gotta properly motivate a woman."

Drake craned his neck at the door. "All right. When you see one let me know. I'll jump right on it."

She dumped the tray on his lap a little too hard. "You're not jumping on anything, Drakey."

She closed the door and switched on the air conditioning. Drake took a mouthful of croissant and washed it down with coffee. He watched Alicia eat her breakfast.

"Stop staring at me. Are you bored again?"

"Yeah, I guess. Remember when Dahl went on holiday? He ended up fighting with some cartel. Why can't that happen to us?"

"I guess we're not lucky that way. Still, we're both half-naked and we can compare war wounds. Again."

Drake smiled in speculation. "We've been in a few good scraps, haven't we, love?"

"Yeah. Even with each other. The sunshine has a way of healing, though."

Their recent bruises, wounds and scrapes inflicted during the escape from Devil's Island and all the adventures before had healed faster under the Caribbean sun. Before that mission, the team had decided to take a step back, to recuperate and revitalize before the endless, dangerous operations they undertook as the SPEAR team got them killed through exhaustion. Hayden had come up with an idea, a proposal. They'd already saved President Coburn's life more times than they cared to remember so Hayden's words were heard almost immediately.

She suggested that they dismantle Team SPEAR and change the format. Instead of utilizing dozens of teams to take on every threat that reared up, they would save crews like SPEAR for the worst-case scenarios. They would be able to rest and revitalize in between, which was reward for everything they'd accomplished during the last five years. But when the time came to act, they would have to perform.

Hayden took to calling the special teams Strike Forces, so Team SPEAR became Strike Force One. The team reluctantly went their separate ways three days later to see how they coped with real life and real relationships.

Drake and Alicia were bored after three days. They visited New Orleans and then California. They checked in with the others every thirty-six hours. Some were faring better than others. Hayden and Kinimaka were doing well. Dahl not so good. Mai and Luther were far afield, in Tokyo, keeping busy. Kenzie and Dallas were treading dangerous waters, as expected. Molokai came and went, losing contact for weeks and then popping back up as if nothing had happened. Karin and Dino went to ground for a while, barely leaving their DC hotel room. Yorgi, unfortunately, remained in hospital.

There was no fresh news concerning the Blood King or the Devil, two evil individuals at the very top of their hit list. It seemed odd that both men would just vanish, but Drake remembered that Dmitry Kovalenko had squandered years of scheming when his plan to kill the President and the SPEAR team failed and had since acquired twenty low-yield nuclear devices. He also remembered that the contract killer known as the Devil needed to relocate and readjust. There was no doubt they would hear from them again.

After several weeks of nothing, Drake started to question why they remained idle. Ever since he joined the army in his teens and, later, the SAS, prior to joining SPEAR, he'd needed very little rest. The constant action had served only to invigorate him and drive the demons away. It was the same for Alicia, he knew, and Torsten Dahl. The hard part was finding the perfect medium between combat and respite.

And some of the criminals they met, those who escaped, haunted his every waking moment.

Still, Hayden assured them there was nothing sinister about their inaction. She kept tabs on current threats almost every day. Yes, jobs came up. Missions that they would normally have undertaken. But nothing within the scope of their new boundaries. So they walked the beaches, grazed over the buffets and watched a bit of Amazon Prime.

It all seemed alien, and bizarre.

Now, Alicia sat on the bed beside him. "When are we due to fly to DC?"

"Three days' time."

"Wanna go today?"

Drake took in his surroundings—the sumptuous bed, the bright sunshine that seemed in endless supply, the perfectly blue waters and the sandy beach. He thought about the polite waiters and happy fellow tourists. The well-mannered service staff. The only danger here came from eating dodgy food.

"Aye," he said. "I don't feel like I fit in."

"The memories don't help."

Drake looked down. Yes, they'd had some great times with SPEAR, and endlessly good camaraderie, but for every prized memory there were two or three bad ones. And the bad ones always held sway.

"When you have time to think," he said, "to break it down . . . that's when it gets dangerous. You second guess. Every decision. Every mission. You start questioning your actions."

"I guess we weren't meant to be tourists," Alicia said.

"We weren't meant to be fighting-robots either."

Alicia gave him a grin. "That actually sounds cool, but I know what you mean."

Drake studied his attire, the incongruous flip-flops on the floor. "Y'know, I find it hard even to socialize with normal people. When a guy passes me on the beach or along the corridor and says 'hi,' I find myself struggling for the proper response. Do I repeat what they said, or do I go for something more in-depth?"

"I guess it's gonna take some readjustment. Fitting in, I mean."

"Not sure that I want to, love."

"Well, what do you want?"

He turned to study those deep, experienced eyes. It was a great question. This was limbo. It wasn't real work and it wasn't actual relaxation. He felt like he was playing a role, forcing himself into some semblance of normality. Or abnormality.

What was the answer?

"I don't know," he said honestly. "We can't work, fight and chase criminals flat out all year round. Maybe you're right . . . maybe it'll take time."

He reached out for the top of her bikini bottoms, just managing to brush the material before she slapped his hand away.

"Careful," she said. "You touch those without consent again and you'll be minus some fingers."

"Aw, come on." He flapped once more but she grabbed his wrist, twisted it, and jumped on top of him. For a moment she stared down into his eyes, straddling him, the heat rising between their bodies.

"Is that a gun in your shorts, Drakey?"

"Does it feel like a gun?"

She reached down. "Not sure. It could be a .45mm."

"Hey!" He rolled on top of her, but she used his momentum against him. He fell off the bed, hitting the floor with a crunch. "Ow, my spine."

Alicia laughed. "There you go. Does that feel more like a working day?"

"Only if you punch me in the face too."

Alicia drew back. Drake grabbed her hips and pulled her forward so that she sat upright in his lap. "I'll pass on the punch," he said. "Let's do something else instead."

For once in her life, Alicia did as she was asked.

They landed in DC a few days later, returning to the same hotel rooms they'd been living out of for the last few years. It hadn't occurred to either of them to start looking for a proper place, at least not that they spoke of. The thought of buying a home to share was an odd one at this stage. Privately, Drake thought they'd vacationed so long that they wouldn't have to face a new problem—where and how the hell would they start living together? Still, they showered and changed and met at a local coffee shop to check for any new updates.

The whole team shared a page where they could study the latest missions, which were rated by color. Red flags would signify a Strike Force event, although they could choose any of the others. The closest they'd come was amber, one down from red, of which there had been two this week. Drake and Alicia read through them whilst sipping hot coffee.

"Looks like someone found the Amber Room," Drake said. "I'd have liked to be in on that."

"Yeah," Alicia agreed. "But you can see why it wasn't a red-flag event. By the time the alert was raised they just needed to secure the area."

Drake nodded. Another parameter Strike Force faced was coming in at the beginning of any mission. Of course, enormous, imminent danger might change that. This time around, their purview wasn't limited in any way. It wasn't just relics, artifacts and old gods. It wasn't just the Blood King or the Devil, although both those individuals were at the top of the list. They could be sent to any incident, anywhere in the world.

"The other amber event," he said, "is still emerging. Based on long-lost artifacts and papers concerning Nikola Tesla."

"We've encountered him before."

"Oh, yeah, he's an interesting guy. Can't imagine why Hayden would decline this one. Especially since it says here—" he tapped at the screen "—that several parties linked to both the Blood King and the Devil have shown interest through known contacts."

"Why don't we ask her?" Alicia plucked a cellphone from her pocket.

Drake nodded and sat back, but as Alicia went to dial, both their phones rang.

CHAPTER THREE

Kenzie ducked low before the tattooed man saw her, falling onto her elbows and feeling a spike of pain.

She came face to face with Dallas.

"All good?" he asked.

"Did you see me dive for cover?"

"Yeah, but that's not unusual for you."

Kenzie ignored him and monitored the rest of the team behind them. They were eight strong, fully loaded, all wearing camouflage gear, all with the customary black grease marks across their faces, all with grim, determined expressions. She tapped the comms system in her right ear.

"Listen up. I see ten goons, all armed. Main targets are the two men standing by the sarcophagus. They're finalizing their deal and are covered by four potentially capable bodyguards. We ready?"

One man replied swiftly, "Are there any . . . swords around?"

Kenzie sighed. "No. Don't worry. No swordplay today."

Relief crossed many faces, including Dallas's.

Kenzie counted three seconds down with her fingers, then they were running, up and over the mound of earth they were using for concealment. Five goons went down immediately, shot through their chests.

A falling automatic weapon discharged by accident, the slug narrowly missing one of Kenzie's companions. Within seconds she was past the earth mound and running on concrete, toward the sarcophagus and the small plane that waited behind it.

Darkness made it harder to keep track of the two bosses

when they split, and their bodyguards that dropped down and returned fire. Kenzie killed one and then sprayed the plane with bullets. No way were these assholes going to escape tonight.

On leaving SPEAR, Kenzie had chosen to go it alone, returning to Israel and then traveling to Egypt. Dallas had tagged along with her, not for any reasons other than they respected each other and didn't want to be alone. Kenzie fought to forget Torsten Dahl and the feelings she had for him. Dallas avoided as many flights, boat rides and coach journeys as he could because, typically, they made him ill. At first, they didn't check in with Hayden and the others or look at the joint webpage where they could see their mission status or keep an eye on any new jobs that might come in. For weeks, they had no ties, no responsibilities, and no danger.

Kenzie grew bored. She fought her true inclinations, which called for a return to the relic smuggling business. But she'd been pardoned of all crimes. This was a clean sheet. Most of her wanted it to stay that way, but there was that rebellious part, that dark side that didn't care.

She had a vast network of connections through Europe and the Middle East, and it was through this that she heard of a new elite task force being set up by the Egyptians, a task force whose sole purpose was to stop valuable, ancient relics leaving the region. Conversely, she'd been initially warned about the task force, but soon decided to approach it with the idea of joining up. Her experience, the contact network and her connection to SPEAR made her the ideal candidate. Dallas had joined her. It turned out the operations were simple raid and assault missions. The job of tracking the relic smugglers down was undertaken by someone else.

It kept Kenzie busy. It kept her mind off Dahl and the rest of the team. It kept her in shape and on the edge. She was too young to take an extended break, she told herself. In truth, there were too many demons railing at her brain. She couldn't bear the thought of confronting them.

The task force started well, thwarting three out of three smuggling operations and suffering only two casualties, both just scrapes. They were so good, in fact, that word spread, and criminals became wary. The task force's fourth assault was an ambush. They barely escaped with their lives, mostly thanks to Kenzie and Dallas, but two of their team were hospitalized and another lost his hearing. Nevertheless, the team continued to operate, getting savvier and even more deadly. In three months, they took out seven long-term smuggling enterprises.

Of course, success resulted in more danger. The gangs increased in number and carried deadlier weapons. Surveillance and infiltration attempts rose. The task force was given no extra resources, just told to get on with it by politicians more concerned about their own appearance.

Now, she stayed low and raced around the plane, just in time to see the two bosses having a confrontation of their own. Guns were out and aimed. A blond man fired first, blowing the other man's brains all over the plane's fuselage. Kenzie shot him in the stomach before rolling underneath the fuselage in an attempt to escape his bodyguard's return fire. Dallas was in concealment behind the wheel. He darted out then and fired two shots that took the bodyguard out. She rolled back the way she'd come, and took stock of the situation.

Only two smugglers remained standing. Two bodyguards were trapped behind some crates, unaware of what had happened to their bosses. A grenade looped toward them

THE FABERGÉ HEIST

and then exploded, ending their involvement. After that the remaining goons surrendered. Kenzie rose, dusted herself off, and took a close look at the sarcophagus.

"Break it open," she told Dallas. "Carefully."

He nodded. Kenzie saw a flicker of movement underneath the plane, dropped and saw the boss she'd shot crawling for a discarded weapon. She shook her head, aimed and fired. There was no directive saying they had to bring back these assholes alive.

Dallas opened the sarcophagus, which was standing upright. A collection of guns, ammo and grenades slithered out. One of the grenades rolled right past Dallas and struck Kenzie's boot before it stopped, making her wince.

"What did I say? Careful."

"Was hardly my fault." Dallas nodded at the plane. "There should be another eight sarcophagi on there."

"Let's check."

The task force's team leader, a man called Duke, was calling everyone together, ready to assault the rear of the plane. Inside were at least four guards and a pilot, but nobody was sure of the greeting they would get. Kenzie fell in behind three other men, Dallas at her side. She found herself thinking about their relationship, which was a strange one.

Dallas liked her and wanted more. He never once tried to hide or deny it. She respected him for that. But no matter how hard she tried, she was still hooked up on the mad Swede. The problem was, she believed Dahl and his wife, Johanna, would split. It was just a matter of time. And she wanted to be there for him. She knew he liked her. But back to Dallas, and his vibrant, humorous, occasionally geeky personality, and she wondered why the hell she didn't give it a go.

The old Kenzie would have. Several times by now.
What the hell has happened to me?

Duke ran around the rear of the plane, gun positioned comfortably in his shoulder. Shots rang out. Kenzie's team rallied around Duke, firing into the back of the plane. Screams and shouts emerged.

Kenzie came up just as a huge, bald man with a white beard leapt out of the plane, a knife in each hand, bellowing and leaking blood from a bullet wound to the right bicep.

He smashed down hard into one of her teammates, crushing him to the floor. The impact was hard, stunning both men, but the massive brute recovered first. Kenzie saw him slide the knife through her colleague's ribcage a second before she hit him, barging him away.

He rolled and came up slashing with both knives, filled with bloodlust and probably some high-grade heroin judging by the wild glare in his eyes. Kenzie caught the first knife on the barrel of her gun, deflecting it. The second knife swung in from her right, which she stepped inside of.

Now she was nose to nose with the big man.

His yelling filled the space around them. His teeth were bared and grinding so loud she heard them over the chaos. She headbutted him, but the helmet she wore spoiled the blow, only serving to confuse him.

Bullets rifled his frame from the side, making him jerk. Kenzie stepped back, pulled her handgun, and shot him between the eyes.

She dropped down beside the man who'd been knifed.

"Cole," she leaned over. "Cole, hang in there."

He was coughing, white-faced. Blood pooled across the floor. Kenzie removed his jacket whilst another man readied a field dressing. Within seconds they had him bandaged, but he didn't look good. Duke, Dallas and the others climbed aboard the plane and made sure it was safe before jumping back out.

"Evac," Duke said. "Right now."

"He needs medevac," Kenzie said.

"He'll get it as soon as we're out of here."

Backup was on its way, waiting to secure the whole area. The task force's job was only to make it safe.

Kenzie had seen this process work before. They hefted Cole and exfilled, jogging for eight minutes before reaching their vehicles and checking on the medevac team. It was three minutes out. Cole would be fine.

Kenzie sat with her back to one of the truck's big wheels, checking her weapons, armor and communications equipment. On one previous occasion, they'd gone straight from one op to the next, with no time to prep. She wouldn't be caught out like that again.

She missed the old team. She missed the camaraderie. The liveliness between Alicia and Mai. The banter between Drake and Dahl. And all the others. She wished this was their op now, and that they were here. When she joined the elite task force she'd called Hayden and the others out of courtesy, in case she couldn't join some of the future ops. To a person, the team had been shocked. They hadn't believed she was working on the right side of the law and had treble-checked everything.

"I think I'd know if I was working for a false flag organization," she'd told them, meaning some criminal organization purporting to be a government agency. Also, she'd floated the possibility that her new team might be able to offer her old team a few jobs, every now and again. The response had been positive.

Dahl had sounded the most concerned. Six weeks ago, he'd even flown out to check on what the elite team were doing. It was a subdued reunion, marred by the fact that they hadn't kept in touch. She didn't know where he stood in his life, and he wasn't sure about hers. They broke the ice over beers and then went on a mission together. Dahl had been a welcome addition to the group. She remembered with fondness one of their conversations.

"Want me to take out that tank?" he'd asked Duke.

"That's a working tank," Duke had replied with incredulity. "Not a reproduction. And it's filled with enemy soldiers."

Dahl had looked confused. "I know."

"You want to take out a tank by yourself?"

"That's what I do."

The mad Swede had proceeded to do just that, reveling in the action, backed up by three men and Kenzie. After that they'd drawn close again, pulled together by the battle heat and the wind-down before Dahl remembered that he had to go home and resume normality.

"Ball and chain still dragging you down?"

"She's not the bad guy here. I guess we all are. Well, I am. The ones that come off worse are the kids."

"If it's not right, they'll get hurt anyway."

Dahl stared at her. "Did you read that on a cereal box?"

"Hey, I've lived too. I know the harsh reality of a failed relationship. Nobody wins. Everyone loses."

"Well, nobody's lost yet."

Dahl returned to Washington, once again vowing to patch up his marriage and do his best for the children. Kenzie hadn't heard from him since.

Now, as Cole was treated by the medevac team and Dallas drank from a fresh bottle of water, Kenzie reflected on everything that had happened since the SPEAR team disbanded. It hadn't helped her, but it had been necessary.

The trouble was, you couldn't just say "I'm gonna spend three months dealing with all the bad shit and then I'll be fine." You couldn't exorcise your demons on demand. It took time, and it took work. As far as she knew the others were all doing well. Maybe it was time to check in with them.

At that moment, her cellphone rang. Before she even looked at the screen Kenzie knew exactly what it would say: *Strike Force One.*

It was the number Hayden had set up for when she needed to call them all together. It was a new mission. Kenzie felt her heart lift and a surge of excitement rush through her.

About bloody time.

CHAPTER FOUR

Hayden and Kinimaka traveled a lot. They started in northern England, visiting Manchester, Harrogate, York and Leeds. The weather wasn't good, but they stayed indoors or used umbrellas or spent entire days in cinemas, watching the latest releases and catching up on old ones. Hayden found comfort in the dark anonymity of a movie theatre. In there, in the dark, where the big screen filled everyone's senses, you didn't have to be anyone. You didn't have to try. Or fight. Or run. Or worry. You could escape.

They drove a lot too. The scenery was often obscured by drizzle, by cloud and fog, but sometimes, they chanced upon bright scenes of natural beauty, found a place to stop, and ate sandwiches and drank coffee, observing the landscape.

It was a getaway. A wind down. Just two people comfortable in each other's company clearing the last few years of chaos from their hearts and souls. Trying to find a way to live with it. They both knew it would take years rather than months, but it was a start.

At nights they found a hotel or a bed and breakfast, took heavy rucksacks up to their rooms and enjoyed some alone time. They both commented how strange it felt. They both found it hard to engage in small talk, not knowing how to properly respond to an idle observation. The immediacy of the chase had been replaced by a lethargy of inactivity.

One night, after two weeks, Kinimaka joined Hayden in her room and they spent hours talking. It was like old times. It wasn't awkward, all the bad was behind them. The next night they spent in one bed, catching up a different way.

"Has there been anyone since me?" Kinimaka asked the next morning.

"Are you kidding? I've been racing around the world with you." She frowned a little. "Why? Has there been with you?"

"Oh yeah." Mano smiled. "I've fallen for many women. But only by tripping over them."

Hayden laughed and tried to roll him onto his back. Her legs were already trying to straddle him when he said, "Do you think there's any future in a relationship like ours?"

Hayden stopped, surprised. "What does that mean?"

"This R&R time is fleeting. It's transient. Soon, we'll be running off again somewhere. In battle. Maybe beaten and tortured. Maybe fighting for our friends like on Devil's Island. The Blood King and the Devil are still out there."

Hayden raised an eyebrow. "So, what do you mean?"

"I guess I'm trying to warn you that we'll never be able to leave the soldier's life."

"Would you want to? Work a steady job? Commute? Trade comfort and safety for living on the edge? For that feeling of exhilaration that comes with every single mission?"

"No," Mano admitted. "But I don't want to lose you again."

Hayden nodded. She agreed to a point, but also felt a little crowded by his depth of emotion. She'd joined the CIA and then SPEAR to help those that couldn't help themselves, to serve, to protect every civilian around the world that struggled to work and provide for their children and pay crippling government taxes that were mostly squandered. She'd joined to help.

"New team," she said. "New life. New missions and new battles. Let's see how it goes first."

Kinimaka nodded and then pulled her on top of him. Unfortunately, he pulled too hard and sent her flying off the side of the bed. Hayden landed with a grunt and two new bruises.

"Shit," she said. "Who needs to fight bad guys when I've got you?"

They continued their tour of England, heading south, stopping on the outskirts of Milton Keynes that night in a large hotel. Hayden took her laptop with them to dinner and made her daily assessment of the new Strike Force initiative. In addition to the always available Internet HQ, there was a red-alert signal that could be sent to their phones if something imminent and terrible happened. Hayden logged into a secure website that was still in the early days of planning.

"A virtual HQ." Kinimaka shook his head. "All those years of trying to find the right headquarters and we end up using a friggin' laptop."

"It's clever." Hayden spun the machine half toward him. "See . . . the inter-agency chatter comes up here." She pointed at several lines of scrolling communications where questions were asked, replied to, and information was shared. "This is the alerts page." She tapped an icon. "It goes blue if there's a new one, green it's been taken, or red if it hasn't. See? There are two new ones now."

"But what if nobody takes them?" Mano asked.

"It doesn't work like that. Other teams are already responding. Units like SWAT, SEALS or Special Ops, depending on the situation. The Strike Force teams are backup until they arrive; then they assume control. In any case, if we have to attend, we get a mobile alert." She opened information regarding the two new missions as Kinimaka looked on.

"A rumble in the jungle in the Amazon," she said. "A European archaeological expedition has been kidnapped by . . . well, they're guessing some drug lord or other. Then there's a Russian oligarch hitting a Syrian oil pipeline. Putin's denying everything, naturally, so the people that really run his country can get richer." She frowned. "I mean what can ten billion buy you that eight billion can't? What drives these people?"

"An extra large yacht?" Kinimaka suggested. "A new hotel? A small country? Who knows?"

Hayden watched the feed for a while, ordering her mains as she waited. "The British are all over the pipeline," she said. "And Trent is covering the Amazon mission. Remember him?"

Kinimaka frowned in surprise. "Trent, Radford and Silk? The disavowed guys? They're part of a Strike Force team now?"

"Yeah, our opposite number actually. They work from the west coast. It's a big team, eighteen strong, so I guess they rotate regularly. Maybe we'll come across them again one day."

"Hope so." Kinimaka looked up eagerly as his meal arrived. Hayden closed the laptop, knowing there'd be no interest from him now until the food was eaten.

Later, she told Kinimaka that all the information placed on the Internet HQ came from a man they were calling the Strike Force coordinator. His codename was G, and nobody knew why. During their months apart, Hayden spoke often to Drake and Dahl, and also to Mai and Luther. They didn't meet, purely because they were traveling so extensively, but heard about other team meetings at far-flung places of the globe.

In the first month, Mai and Luther met Molokai in Hong

Kong. It was quick, but it was comforting, they said. Catching up set them at ease and showed that everyone else was feeling the same way as they were, which was slightly lost.

In the second month, Dahl joined Karin and Dino, and later Kenzie, over in the Middle East. Both meetings were good, fruitful. Dahl reported that all members of the team were still very much in shape and eager to jump into new missions. Dahl himself seemed quiet to Hayden, even over the phone. The Swede had a lot on his mind.

"This Strike Force coordinator," Kinimaka said, one rainy day in England. "What does he do exactly?"

"He's a go-between for several different agencies, national and international. CIA. FBI. Interpol. MI6. Trusted contacts. He gets up to the minute information. He has a vital job on his hands."

"And he knows an awful lot," Kinimaka stated.

"I guess so." Hayden nodded. "Are you saying he could become compromised?"

Kinimaka shrugged. "It's something to bear in mind with everything we know about the Blood King."

As their vacation drew to a close, they decided to head back to DC to find a place to live. The excitement of apartment hunting preoccupied them for a while. They spoke to Drake and also to Kono, Mano's sister, who was now living just a half-hour drive from them. It didn't occur to Kinimaka to arrange a meeting until Hayden prompted him, but once he organized it, they lunched at the Hard Rock together and found out Kono was expecting a baby to her new husband—a man called Hanini, or Han for short, which according to Kinimaka meant "to pour down like rain" in Hawaiian.

"Not sure about the name," Mano said. "But I'll love the baby. Congrats, sis!"

Hayden found it all so incredibly atypical for her. This was actual life, real people building a present and a future. This was what she protected, and it was great to see and hear it working first hand.

Still, she wanted more.

"I think we should go back to Hawaii," Kinimaka said. "Just for a short time, and not necessarily alone. I'd love to go with the team."

"Agreed." Hayden had a soft spot for Mano's homeland and loved the atmosphere of the Pacific state.

They settled into their new apartment, bought furniture, even looked at the possibilities of cooking food. Kinimaka was predictably great at it; Hayden not so good.

But she always reminded herself that, whether they were burning food or ordering takeaway, they weren't being shot at or chasing the worst kind of human detritus.

After Mano's latest creation in the kitchen, a scoop of rice, some chicken laulau, a helping of poi and coconut cream pudding for dessert, Hayden settled back with a glass of wine in her hand, flipped up the laptop and checked that day's reports.

And found the new mission.

CHAPTER FIVE

Torsten Dahl knew the end was coming. The kids loved having him home, but Johanna didn't. She'd seen too much, experienced too much of his world, and couldn't understand why he chose to remain there.

"He was behind me," she said late one night. "He touched me. He could have murdered me, and the kids, and I wouldn't have known anything about it. I can't live with that failure, that incompetence. I have to believe that I can at least try to save my kids if someone threatens them."

She was talking about the world's most ruthless and brilliant contract killer. A man known as the Devil. It seemed Luka Kovalenko—the new Blood King—had put out a contract on Dahl's family which the Devil had initially taken on. It was only later, after the Blood King tried to erase the Devil in nuclear fire, that the contract killer changed his mind. Still, he'd come horrifically close.

"Why would you choose a life that can come back and threaten your family?" Johanna asked.

She didn't understand then and she never would. He'd tried many times to explain his calling, his passion, the natural abilities that suited a soldier's lifestyle. He'd tried to explain that he didn't love her any less. He couldn't explain the trauma of battle in the same way he couldn't explain the unease he felt when walking around a shopping mall.

He felt far more comfortable stalking through an enemy encampment.

"It's not a choice," he said, "when you can't do anything else."

That made her frustrated and angry. But he didn't mean

he was incapable of doing anything else. He meant being a soldier was his one vocation.

"Can you promise me nothing like that will ever happen again?"

He couldn't, and that was the worst of it. With people like Kovalenko and the Devil at large it was never going to be safe. He'd been forced to explain to her what the Devil did and how he did it. His past exploits. Johanna had found it hard to believe such people existed.

"Who would bring down an entire airliner to kill one person? Who would blow up a house to kill a single woman? Who would engineer a riot at a parade to kill a wife and two children?"

"It's his occupation," Dahl had said.

"No," she'd spat at him. "It's his vocation."

The days with the kids were small slices of heaven. It was only on these days that he managed to relax. Weeks went by. He kept in touch with Drake and Hayden, and kept abreast of Kenzie's exploits, fully expecting her to revert to some clandestine, underworld activity. It was with disbelief that he heard she and Dallas had joined a task force whose job it was to track down relic smugglers. He even found himself wondering if she was working undercover, making sure the smugglers got away. But he didn't really believe that, and she proved him right.

When things became difficult at home, Dahl took a trip. He went to see Kenzie, not just to see how things lay between them but to observe her new operation. It looked good. The team had gained some valuable victories.

During the visit when he'd joined one of their missions, he'd felt free again. It told him everything he needed to know.

Dahl returned to Washington, miserably certain he

needed to finalize things with Johanna. But it was the weekend. The children were off school and demanded all his attention. He was happy to oblige. Another two days went by before he talked to Johanna.

He didn't have to explain anything. Johanna had already seen it on his face.

"I tried so hard," she said. "Followed you to America. Explained night after night to the children why you weren't there for them. I can do anything for them, but I can't save them from professional killers."

"You shouldn't have to," Dahl said. "You three mean the world to me. But I can't see you unhappy. Trapped. We're different people to the ones that married years ago. We haven't grown together. You need to look to yourself as well as the kids."

There was very little else to say. They decided to explain it to the children together, and Dahl knew it would be one of the hardest nights of his life.

Now, four weeks later, they had gone. Dahl was alone days and nights, alone in an apartment that now echoed with silence as loudly as it had once echoed with the voices of his children. It was a terrible, deep silence, bereft of all joy. Who knew the sound of a child's voice could bring so much life to a place? It was only when they were gone that you understood.

He spent nights checking the digital HQ, scrutinizing jobs and wishing Hayden would take one of them. Several looked promising. There was everything from robberies to a small war, but their hiatus continued. Dahl realized he was finding it harder to rest than to fight.

Days were spent keeping in shape, staying close to the edge of where he needed to be. He spoke to Johanna and the kids, to Drake and Hayden. They asked him to join them for a while. He told them he needed to get back to work.

"It's gonna take time, mate," Drake told him. "All this R&R bollocks. It takes some getting used to. But you know as well as anyone, we couldn't stay at the level we were. Friends have died along the way, and maybe it was because we never took a fucking break."

Dahl thought about that. He didn't believe it and neither did Drake. "That's not true and you know it."

"Maybe. Listen, we're headed back to DC soon. How about Alicia and I surprise you, blindfold you, take you to some alley and kick the shit out of you?"

"Sounds bloody perfect. Thanks, Drake. I really need something like that to perk me back up."

"It's a deal."

"Just . . . don't let Alicia shag me. The kicking will be torture enough."

"Piss off, Torsty!" Alicia cried in the background.

They ended the call. Dahl's outlook improved. It felt good to connect with the team again. Maybe if they saw each other, even socially, it wouldn't be so bad.

His phone rang five minutes later. He knew the ring tone and when he checked the screen it read: *Strike Force One*.

Hallelujah!

CHAPTER SIX

Karin and Dino took Mai's advice. They found a room in DC and rarely surfaced for the first two weeks. They lost track of time. They emerged only for food, grabbing takeaways, supermarket essentials and snacks, sometimes not knowing if it was early morning, late evening or the middle of the day. Karin enjoyed the closeness, the passion, and the diversity of it all until the newness started to wear off. Time passed by in a blur after that. Every day blended into the next. They kept in touch but barely remembered which day of the week it was.

"I don't know if I can do this," she said during the third month.

"What?" Dino sat up in bed, his dark half-Italian features scrunched in concern, his short black hair sticking up in tufts.

"I don't mean us," Karin clarified. "I mean this."

Dino continued to frown.

"The downtime."

"I guess. We only just became soldiers and thank God we escaped the deserter charge. But it's not like it is for the other guys. Fighting is all they've ever known. Especially Alicia. Didn't she leave home at sixteen or so, to join the Army?"

"Something like that."

"It's harder for them."

"I guess. Most of them feel the same. But that doesn't make me feel any different."

Dino pulled the covers around him. "So now you've gotten lucky you want to go back to war?"

"Gotten lucky?" Karin raised an eyebrow at him. "I'd say you were the one that got lucky."

"You're kidding, right? Have you seen this body and felt what it can do?"

Karin shook her head. "You're a knobhead, you know that?"

Dino reached out for a half-drunk bottle of water. "All right. Seriously, what do you want?"

Karin arranged her pillows behind her back and sat up straight, hugging the top sheet to her neck. Finally, it seemed, Dino was sincere.

"What do I want?" she echoed, thinking. "Well, a lot has changed since I joined up. Since Komodo died." She was silent for a long time, remembering the love of her life and the happy, respectful relationship they'd shared.

"I want to help," she said in the end. "Not just our countries, our people. But my friends. I want to make a difference so that when it's my time to retire I can look back and say—I helped. They say the noblest art is that of making others happy. Well, the greatest art is making others feel safe."

Dino threw the covers aside. "I guess we didn't expend all that blood, sweat and tears training for nothing. We know we've got skills, so let's use them."

Galvanized, Karin felt a surge of enthusiasm. She knew what she wanted. She knew where she wanted to be. There was only one problem.

"We don't have a job."

"Eh? I didn't know we needed one."

"No, I don't mean a job. I mean a mission. We're stuck here until Hayden chooses a new one."

Dino sat back, deflated. "Shit."

Karin broke out the laptop. They'd checked the new HQ

regularly but had relied on their cellphones for crucial updates. She took a moment to scrawl through the chatter and ops that had been turned down.

"At least two we could have sunk our teeth into."

"Maybe we could join one of the other Strike Forces," Dino suggested. "I mean three and four look pretty active."

Karin looked up when her phone rang. Dino caught her eyes. "Wow," he said. "I shoulda said that before."

Molokai drifted. He hired a car and followed a route that took him across the center of North America. Weeks passed. He enjoyed it. He was used to being the loner. The big coat and the robes he wore to spare the public's feelings were washed and then replaced. Molokai didn't continue wearing them because he felt embarrassed or conspicuous. He wore them to save others from seeing the old welts and scars that crisscrossed the lower part of his face, neck and shoulders. He ignored the looks, suffered the attention of the cops when they stopped him, and proceeded to lose himself.

Molokai drove in a western direction, never knowing which town he was passing or where he would end up. It was about as free as he could get. Every day he checked the Internet HQ, wondering if another mission would pop up but never sure he wanted to be part of this team. To date, he'd been caught in an irrepressible flow. One job led to another and the danger never let up. Luther was fully invested, but then Luther had Mai.

Molokai ended up in San Francisco. He spent some days wandering the city, took a tourist trip he enjoyed over to Alcatraz, and watched what remained of the seals in the harbor. He walked in the rain, helped a pair of cops out of some trouble with a local gang, and then decided to take a longer trip.

He flew to Tokyo to see Mai and Luther. It was a good few days, and took his mind off things. He even managed to open up about a part of his past he hated, and although the conversation merely skirted the subject it was a therapeutic start.

"He was the best bomb tech of the Iraq War," Luther told Mai late one night to Molokai's surprise. "Never broke a sweat."

Molokai was surprised to find himself expanding on that. "Five years, four tours, I didn't have to hide anything there. I was a soldier, among soldiers. The men I met were outstanding. They still are . . . the ones that returned."

They talked and talked. Molokai usually avoided the subject because it always came down to one fateful day, but after two hours of healing conversation he was almost ready to discuss it.

"October 2010," he said. "My final tour. The cost of the war was into trillions by then, mostly because it was financed on borrowed money, but they didn't have enough funds to outfit our troops properly. Our weapons were over-used, our equipment always breaking. They lost Abrams tanks like children lose toys. Anyway, an IED was reported close to a checkpoint. It turned out to be an artillery shell to which a detonating mechanism had been attached. Nothing fancy, but incredibly volatile. I went over, got to work. They didn't disturb me because they knew I needed my space, some soft music on the earphones, and time to breathe. It turned out to be a diversion. Whilst I worked, four snipers took out eight friends and I never even knew. Didn't hear the commotion."

"You were doing your job," Luther said, big fist clenched in concern.

"Sure, and so were the insurgents. It turned out that I lived, eight of our number died and, when I joined the fight, they blew up the IED anyway, injuring two more. The rest of the war went by in a blur."

Molokai found the events hard to discuss, and just as hard to reflect on. He kept moving after that, soon leaving Tokyo and returning to the US.

When the cellphone call came he was incredibly relieved.

CHAPTER SEVEN

When Mai Kitano landed in Tokyo, both she and Luther were still sore and bruised from their escape from Devil's Island. Not only that, they were mentally tormented by losing both the Blood King and the Devil, agonized to know that two such extreme dangers still walked the earth like malevolent monsters.

Since London though, since they were attacked in the Knightsbridge restaurant and thrown headlong into death and hellfire, they had both sporadically wondered the same thing.

Where would that night have ended up?

Mai knew Luther thought about it, because he told her so. Outside of an ongoing op, she was more reserved and preferred to choose her words carefully. Especially when she was with a guy she didn't know that well. Her relationship with Drake had been different. They'd met under fire and when they were much younger, which made it easy to get into each other's life stories. Now, she was older; she'd been to hell and back. And she didn't want to make another mistake.

It turned out Luther felt the same way. Beneath the larger than life exterior he was quite the thinker.

They agreed to repeat the early part of that fateful London night, found a restaurant in Tokyo, and a table in the corner. Only days had passed since they split from the team and they hadn't checked the Internet HQ out yet. They had more important decisions to make.

"Where's this going?" Mai asked bluntly, having done all her thinking on the plane journey. "What do you see?"

"A steak," Luther said. "Definitely a steak. No garlic butter though. I wouldn't want it to come between us later."

Mai waited. She knew him well enough to have expected the standard response. Now she watched him thinking about the question.

"I see a start," he said finally, struggling to keep his voice at a lower level. "A chance to get to know each other properly. And I don't think . . ." He paused but then continued, "I really don't think we're gonna get a better chance."

"Why not?"

"I don't mean with other people. I mean for this relationship. The team's new initiative means we can recuperate between missions. It means we can have a life too. It means we don't have to go relic hunting every week but can choose a wide variety of missions. Who knows what diverse and wonderful ops might come up?" He shrugged and grinned. "But that's digressing. We now have time to think, to process, to make up our minds over weeks and months rather than days. I say, let's take it steady and see where we are tomorrow. Next week. Next month."

It was exactly what Mai wanted to hear, and it clearly came from the heart. Three hours later they were throwing back the covers of a double bed on the third floor of an expensive hotel room. Luther again checked she was okay with it, but that only made her jump at him. She was fast, but he managed to catch her, holding her up with his large arms as she wrapped her legs around his waist.

"Stop checking with me," she whispered. "If I didn't want this, you'd definitely know about it. Are you nervous?"

Luther coughed. "Well, it's been a while."

"Ah, well try to keep up. I'll teach you as we go."

"Hey, it's not been that long!"

They damaged the room a little, spending fun-filled, exhausting hours losing themselves in each other. They ordered room service and called Chika and Dai, Mai's sister and her boyfriend, to tell them they'd be late. They were expecting to stay at Chika's house that night but didn't turn up until three days later.

And still, they took it steady.

Luther left for a couple of days, heading out to visit some army buddies at a nearby US base. It was little more than a barracks, a bare-bones base, but Luther wouldn't pass up getting reacquainted with a couple of old friends, men he'd shared action with. The time he spent with them tempered his happiness when he learned about colleagues lost and injured on the field of battle. It was with a wrench that he left them two days later, but he greeted Mai with a smile when he met her at Chika and Dai's front door.

"Hey."

She pulled him inside and introduced him to her sister and old friend. Both Mai and Luther checked in-house security—it would be beefed up until both the Blood King and the Devil were captured or killed—and found it to be top-notch. They even had a panic room.

Mai rang Drake and Hayden every so often, staying in touch. Molokai came to visit. Mai found she understood the reserved outsider a little better.

Almost three months later, Luther and she were fighting each other daily. In the ring, on the mat, keeping fit, staying sharp. Numerous phone calls from various members of the team told an interesting tale. Once the first week of inactivity had passed, they were all raring to go.

She checked on Yorgi who seemed to have lost touch with the team. The young Russian thief was still recovering from being shot in the back. He'd been discharged from hospital but had suffered complications and was being made to undergo a strict protocol of exercise and rest. The prognosis was that he'd be back to normal in two to three months.

What "normal" was Mai didn't know. She read between the lines. She knew how hard it had to be hitting Yorgi. His expertise had been bouldering, climbing where others couldn't. He relied on his total fitness.

And then, one late night as she and Luther were in a deep sleep, her cellphone rang. A rush of adrenaline shot through her. She rolled over but Luther was already holding the phone up, showing her the screen.

"Strike Force One," he said.

She pushed the answer button. "Hello?"

"It's G," a voice said, which she knew belonged to their coordinator. "We have a job. I need you on a plane as soon as possible."

"What job?"

"You'll be briefed when you land. I'll text you the details. It's a hotel in Utah, outside Salt Lake City."

G signed off. Mai blinked at Luther.

"Vacation's over," she said. "Let's get back to work."

CHAPTER EIGHT

On Thursday, Cara drove into Las Vegas with the other members of her team, the One Percenters, the greatest heist team never to be caught. The vibe in the car was ice cold. She hated what Jax had become—a grim, emotionless leader happy to cause unnecessary harm to others—and couldn't understand how it had happened in just a few months. She expected it from Steele, the pair of them had been at loggerheads for many years. But Jax?

Their leader was usually the consummate professional. He came from a Special Forces background, but had always professionally reined in his violent tendencies. He'd always been the voice of reason with overarching perspective, able to see issues as they arose. He was the major reason the team had never been caught or seen beyond a few grainy photographs.

What's happened to him?

Maybe he couldn't help this demise. Steele certainly couldn't. Cara hadn't joined them for the danger, the thrill, or even the money. She was in it for the art of thievery, to see a job perfectly executed. It was the thing that drove her more than anything. Three months ago, when the Fabergé heist had been proposed, she'd fallen under its spell. It sounded legendary, just perfect. She'd been unable to say no. And as they planned, as the team's joint skills blended together into a flawless, beautiful, complete jigsaw, she allowed the excitement to infuse her.

It would be the greatest heist yet.

And it still should be. But . . .

Cara pushed the doubts away. She checked the rearview

mirror, catching a glimpse of her own blond hair and perfect face as she checked out Faye and Kushner. Both looked relaxed. But then they would. Faye was their technical expert; she would always remain remote from the robbery and thus never shoulder any of the risk. Kushner was the consummate thief, probably the best in the world. He rarely thought about anything beyond the upcoming job and his own good looks.

Steele was crammed into the car's far side, glowering back at her, no doubt clenching his fists. Jax was in the passenger seat. She ignored him as they took their time driving the length of Las Vegas Boulevard.

"It's changed a lot since I was last here," he said, staring out the window.

Cara agreed but stayed quiet. There were new hotels, new complexes, new shows and new bridges. New roads. Lots of different ways to exfil after the job. A stadium was being built west of Mandalay Bay that, Faye informed them, would be the new home for the Raiders football team. The construction was huge.

Cara watched all the long-standing hotels and casinos pass by. From Circus Circus at the north, passing Elvis Presley Boulevard, to the Venetian and Treasure Island and her favorite of all: Caesar's Palace. The fountains of Bellagio were in full swing, using over 1,200 nozzles and 4,500 lights to deliver vast, spectacular light shows every half hour, with some of the water blasting almost 500 feet into the air.

They passed Planet Hollywood and, new to all of them, an area fronted by The Crystals, an upscale luxury shopping mall. The MGM, the new Hard Rock Café, and then Excalibur—which had been there as long as she could remember, caught her eye before they turned around opposite the Luxor.

"Drive it again," Jax said. "I couldn't take it all in the first time."

She was already on it but questioned him anyway. "The Strip won't affect our getaway."

"I know that, but do it. Keep your eyes open."

Cara shook her head. His words were bordering on ridiculous, spoken to shut her up so that he could continue to wallow in whatever pit his mind occupied. It didn't worry her that he was being distant.

What worried her was that the artistry of the job might be compromised.

Then, everyone in the car faded away as their target hotel came into view. It was new, nestling slightly behind the MGM Grand, on East Harmon Avenue, but still towering above the Strip and shining its red and gold lights this early on a Thursday. Still, if there was any city in the world that never slept, this was the one.

All five of them beheld their closest view yet of the target hotel: the Azure. Almost 500 feet tall it had cost over 2.5 billion dollars to build, boasted 2500 rooms, a 70,000-square-foot casino, 250,000 square feet of retail and restaurant space, a spa and fitness facility, a 2000-seat cinema complex, and 100,000 square feet of convention space. It had already been rated as the best hotel in the world by Gogobot and the Condé Nast Traveller gold list. It was also the place Lady Gaga, Tom Cruise, and other celebrities stayed when they visited Vegas.

All of the above facts had no doubt attracted the man they were targeting.

Cara found a place to park and waited until they were all together. They walked through the casino, tuning out shouting and laughter and the noise of the machines. They walked the retail and restaurant areas. They ventured as far as they were able without rousing attention. Nothing was different to the blueprints they'd already studied, but it had to be physically checked.

Satisfied, they left.

Kushner stared out the car window, looking up toward the top of the hotel. "Soon," he said with pleasure in his voice. "Very soon."

Cara followed his gaze. "Wish I was going up there with you."

Faye looked shocked. "Really? You know it's 500 feet high, right?"

"Entry is the most skilful part of the job."

Kushner nodded. "Agreed. But I have it covered."

"And I'll be there to smash heads just in case." Steele grinned.

"Just don't smash the eggs," Jax said. "For all our sakes."

Cara narrowed her eyes. Their leader sounded desperate. "Is there something you're not telling us, Jax?"

He shook his head. "Stop being so friggin' paranoid."

Kushner snorted. "We're thieves. Paranoia is how we survive."

"Not with me, you don't. Look, we've pulled off eight epic heists. We're the best in the business. Just stick to the plan."

"Always do." Kushner sat back.

Cara drove between several bus stations for the reminder of the afternoon where they all took turns buying various tickets to Los Angeles for around twenty dollars. The more choice they had the easier it would be, so they covered all of them. It was a tedious job and Kushner didn't like it, but Jax shut him up. As the sun set, Jax and Steele departed to collect some special explosives they'd had prepared and a set of guns and ammo. This part was always delicate, but they later reported it passed almost without incident. Their suppliers had forgotten what Kushner called "his special glass tool," but rather than incite a tense incident he couldn't control, Jax asked Kushner to make one himself. They'd be all right.

Thursday night rolled around. Tonight was important to their plans in laying the groundwork for Saturday. To pass the time they tuned into a police band radio, listening to the chatter. It was only normal to expect the authorities to have heard something about an upcoming raid. No specifics, but due to all the third parties and go-betweens the gang had to use for materials, it was accepted that chatter would get out. Jax further confused them by dropping clues for other imaginary robberies at other dates but the cops weren't as clueless as most people wanted them to be.

All over Vegas, they'd be on alert for something during the next week or so. It was natural. It was expected.

It had been built into their Plan B.

Cara readied herself as Faye fired up two of her state-of-the-art computers and proceeded to hack into the local CCTV network. The slim, wiry geek was using a backdoor she'd created four weeks ago. Cara drove the car to one of the Azure's neighboring high-rises, a place called the Wyndham, which was somewhat shorter, not as grand, and far less security conscious.

Cara, Jax, Steele and Kushner changed their outer appearances with disguises and new clothes. They added implants to their cheeks and donned sunglasses. They wore long coats. Soon they were inside the Wyndham, heading to the roof. With Faye hacking the CCTV they gained access in no time, waiting just thirty seconds for Kushner to breach the final door using a homemade foil device to fool its safety measures.

Up on the roof, Faye again neutralized the single CCTV camera which stood on a tall black pole, scanning the area. The building stood just under 400 feet in height, less than the Azure, but they could still see Las Vegas in all its radiant glory spread out before them. From this angle it looked calm, surreal, an oasis of illumination in the desert. Car lights snaked along the Strip, never ending. The names of Caesar's, the Venetian and Palazzo were radiant beacons. The echoing din of vehicles and humans could be heard as a gentle rumble.

Cara smoothed her hair as a gust of wind blew it out of place. She was looking upward. "The Azure's penthouse is dark."

"I noticed," Kushner said. "Faye, check Mr. Singh arrived as expected."

"On it. Yeah, the Indian billionaire arrived yesterday."

"We'll keep an eye on it," Jax said. "Could be any amount of reasons it's still dark."

Cara measured the distance between the Wyndham and the Azure with a special laser. Everything they'd planned remotely matched up.

"To Saturday then." Kushner grinned.

"Gonna break some hearts," Steele smirked. "And maybe some heads."

Cara turned away from him, hiding her resentment. He made her angry. All her young life she'd been a target, the victim of bullies either because she was too slim or skinny, too beautiful or too blond. Steele was nothing but a privileged bully in her opinion, who'd managed to fall on his feet when he'd met Jax in the military.

"You need to try the gloves," Jax said.

Kushner nodded, slipped on the gripper gloves they'd stolen from the Californian tech lab, and used a rope to lower himself over the far side of the building. The risk was lower there, and the technology needed to be checked.

"Don't fall, man." Steele chuckled. "Without you, it's gonna be a lot harder."

Kushner ignored him. Cara leaned over the edge. A new breeze tousled her hair, but she didn't feel it. She was too engrossed watching Kushner.

Clad in black, moving with arms and legs outspread, he used only the gloves to stick to a large window on the outside of the hotel. His boots were made of thick, rubber pads and, if he put both feet on the glass, they gave reasonable grip, but the only thing keeping him from falling 400 feet to the sidewalk were the new gloves.

They held on to the flat pane firmly. Kushner turned sideways but refrained from performing the full Spiderman routine by turning upside down. Cara watched, drinking in the sounds of the city as the warm night air clung to her. She could smell cooked meat too, which probably meant there was a restaurant below her. Far away, the sound of sirens split the night.

She found herself half-hoping the gloves would fail. Without the gloves the plan was dead. Kushner would be okay—he was still attached to the roof by a rope—but with the new aberration in Jax's temperament and character, she wasn't sure she wanted the job to go ahead.

"Happy with this pair," Kushner reported back. "I'll check out the second."

As he worked, Cara caught Jax staring at her. She glared back, hoping he'd sense her uneasiness. If he did, he gave no outward sign.

Jax contacted Faye. "Anything on the police band?"

"Not really. I guess they know we could be listening. There's an increased presence. All the hotels have beefed up security. Anyone with valuables has been checked out and checked again."

"Including Mr. Singh," Cara said.

"Singh won't know what hit him," Steele said. "And neither will his security. I, for one, can't wait for Saturday night in Vegas."

As the big enforcer moved to the edge of the roof, watching Kushner, Cara found herself several feet back with Jax. She couldn't hold back any longer.

"Are you still with us, Jax?"

He turned angry eyes on her. "What the hell do you mean?"

"I think you know. Something isn't right with you, it hasn't been right for months now. I know you'd never compromise us by wearing a wire. I know you're the driving force behind this crew. But Jax . . . you aren't yourself."

Jax used his right hand to scrape the stubble that covered his scalp. He looked down, signaling nerves. All she wanted him to do was to look her in the eyes.

"I'm stressed, yes. But you can search me if you like. I'm no snitch. My personal life got way complicated recently."

She knew next to nothing about his personal life. It was how they rolled, better for them and the crew in general. Her own life was an enigma to all of them.

"I won't ask you to explain, Jax, but is it gonna affect this job?"

Jax managed to meet her eyes. "No," he said. "This job has to run smoothly. It has to."

Cara nodded. "That sounds pretty desperate. If you need money . . ."

"It's not money."

"We've had a good run, Jax. The best. We took down Dubai in the middle of that horse race. We raided the Covent Garden depository in the middle of the Olympics, a theft that's still never been reported. There's no team on this planet as good as us." She smiled. "And now we're here.

Friggin' Vegas. The biggest of them all. We need you on your A-game."

Jax regarded her, and she saw some of the struggle in his face. It was clear that something was affecting him, and also clear he needed to talk about it. "My head's on straight," he said. "You should know that."

"You're not the man I signed up with. Back then, you were charismatic, thoughtful, as fast as lightning and cleverer than all of us. You've always had a violent background, Jax, but you never resorted to it."

"Life changes." Jax turned away. "It gets hard. Things happen that you never even see coming."

Cara didn't look at him, just continued staring over the impressive, bright cityscape. Out there, dreams were made. Lives were broken. Fortunes were won and lost on the roll of a ball, a card or a machine. Chance was king, pretty much like real life. It was the most desirable adult playground in the world.

"Well, something's not right. And it's not going to get me arrested. You hear me? If I see you falling apart, I'm outta here."

"You won't get arrested, Cara. That much is certain."

He was usually shrewd. The pointers she was getting from him now didn't add up. He seemed almost lost. Desperate.

What the hell was going on?

Jax turned away as Kushner reappeared, slipping over the top of the building. Cara saw the best thief in the world give both pairs of gloves the all clear.

"We're ready then," Jax said. "A bit more planning tomorrow and then it's game on for Saturday."

For the first time in their eight heist history, Cara felt nervous.

CHAPTER NINE

Mr. Singh was a collector. He was born in Kathmandu more than sixty years ago, the son of a bookseller that catered to tourists in the popular travelers' neighborhood of Thamel. Singh had considered himself poor until he saw how some of his friends lived, how they sometimes fought for scraps in the street and got arrested for stealing. Singh spent his days at school or in the shop, tucked in a corner and reading. He attributed his every success to the books he'd read; they had opened his eyes to the world. But he attributed his shrewdness to the travelers he met; the men and women that dropped by the dingy shop and talked freely to the small boy, giving him life tips whether he wanted them or not.

Growing up sitting on the ledge of a square, grime-laden window that looked over tourist-ridden Kathmandu, reading until the sun set. These were his best childhood memories. His parents had been aloof; they provided but showed him no love. When Singh got the chance, he moved to India and started trading.

Businesses followed, making the young man a wise adult. Before he was twenty-two he'd tried his hand at fourteen different business models. Eleven fell flat on their faces but that didn't deter Singh. To him, it meant three worked. That kept him going. Building off failures he started another fourteen and three of those worked. They were small, they didn't bring in much profit, but they kept him in lodgings, food and clothes.

Barely.

The age of twenty-five flew by and then thirty

approached. Singh felt energized, despite struggling every day. He was working for himself, hardly finding time to sleep, remaining a loner because he didn't have free time to socialize. He owned market stalls and warehouses, a small shop and an even smaller bookstore. He avoided the eyes of the criminal fraternities because he was so low-key. They couldn't make money off him. He considered himself a wheeler-dealer, able to buy a box of broken watches and sell them at a profit to a watchmaker, who would do all the hard work of mending them.

At the age of thirty-five, he had been in business for twenty years.

It was then that he started to see some profit, mostly from storage units and warehouses he had procured through the years. They didn't need much maintenance. People simply rented the spaces, using them for whatever they liked. Singh turned eight spaces into sixteen and then forty. Singh gave the people more of what they wanted.

A month before his fortieth birthday, Singh had the idea of not just finding and renting units but building them. From that point on he never looked back. Units became stores and buildings and more. His empire grew until he couldn't see either end of it. It outgrew him. He was fifty when he sold everything for an estimated 1.2 billion dollars.

Singh had lived lavishly ever since. The old drive was tempered. He decided to live a little, to take pleasure in everything that he'd missed whilst building an empire. He took time to find out what he liked in this world, the things that moved him. In the end, the real jewels he found harked back to his childhood.

What fascinated him were mystery stories. And objects surrounded by mystery. He loved relics and old artifacts that couldn't be explained. He delved into their histories, rediscovering the love of reading. He traveled the world to seek them out, to sit and stare at beautiful, mysterious vestiges of the past. Eight years ago, he learned about the Fabergé eggs.

The first egg was crafted for Tsar Alexander III in 1885. Known as the Hen egg it was built on a foundation of gold. Its shell split to reveal a matte yellow-gold yolk, which opened to reveal a multi-colored golden hen which also opened. The hen itself comprised a diamond replica of the imperial crown upon which hung a priceless red ruby. The egg was received with wonder. Fabergé was appointed "goldsmith by special appointment to the imperial crown" and given carte blanche to design all future imperial Easter eggs. They became more elaborate, intricate and ornate.

Singh loved the story of the eggs. They were a genuine manmade treasure, a legacy designed by a man for a queen that would live forever. They weren't made or given for profit, there was no ulterior motive. The story of the eggs enchanted him.

So much so that he didn't leave his mansion for three weeks.

Singh learned everything he could through the Internet, libraries, and old books purchased and delivered to him through intermediaries. He sought out professors well versed in the Fabergé legends, men that had devoted life and lectures to the old family up to 1918 when they were forced out of Russia. The history was fascinating.

Every egg was unique and contained a surprise. Out of the fifty imperial Easter eggs, Nicholas II presented twenty to his wife and thirty to his mother. They became famous. Fabergé was commissioned to make eggs for private clients such as the Duchess of Marlborough and the Rothschild family. Of the fifty imperial Easter eggs, forty-three survived.

Seven were lost.

Singh's brain latched on to this fact and wouldn't let go. Lost, not destroyed. The wording was interesting. That was all it took, and Singh was captivated. Today, it is known where many of the original eggs are—people such as Viktor Vekelsberg, Albert of Monaco and the British royal family owned many. Others were kept at the Kremlin, the Hillwood Museum in Washington DC and the Fabergé Museum in Germany. Some had been taken out of all knowledge, stored by private collectors, and one lived in Qatar. Singh made heartfelt but huge financial offers to as many of these owners as he could find. It took time, it took persistence, but his collection grew.

And as it grew, he searched for the lost eggs.

Singh became obsessed, finding the old drive and channeling it into the new search. At least some of those seven lost eggs were abroad in the world and Singh wanted to find them.

Always, he was conscious that the greatest and largest display of eggs ever to be seen in public totaled nine. It was assembled by Malcolm Forbes, the publisher of *Forbes Magazine*, and shown in New York City.

I know I can beat that, but I want my display to be something special.

Singh strived for four years, living and breathing the lost eggs, chasing down false lead after lead, climbing every imaginary mountain and crossing every literal sea. It reminded him of the battle of his youth, continually pushing for success. He was motivated again, feeling young again. This purpose, this legacy, would hopefully outlive him and give the world something to marvel at. To remember him by. If looking at his collection made them happy, then he had won at life.

With seven lost eggs to find, he was confident he would succeed.

Now, Singh turned on the lights of his suite on the penthouse floor of the Las Vegas Azure hotel and casino. It was the first time he'd been in the lavish set of rooms and it was late. Singh hated social functions but had braced himself for this one through months of preparation. He turned to the black-haired woman who'd accompanied him.

"Thank you so much for your help. Again."

"It's my pleasure, Mr. Singh. I hope I have helped."

"Are you kidding?" He laughed. "I wouldn't be here without you. At least, not in this state of mind." He gave another quick laugh. "Your social coaching has given me the confidence to survive Thursday to Thursday in Las Vegas. What more could I ask?"

"I'm happy that it has given you the confidence to speak in public," she said. "Since that is what I'm paid to do."

"Yes, yes," he said, eager to see what the construction crews were concocting in his suite of rooms. It was unusual for a hotel to redesign their rooms for a simple display, but everything about this event was unusual. Unique. Once in a lifetime.

"I am confident I can get through the events I have to participate in. The speaking parts." He was distracted now. "I have to. I started all this. I must finish it."

But it would all be worth it.

The Fabergé collection was worth it.

The Singh collection, he amended silently.

"I'll leave you alone now."

"Thank you. I will see you in the morning."

He closed the door behind her. He wasn't alone. The

designers were still working, creating the perfect podiums on which to present his incredible collection. The TV crews were setting up. Hotel management was here too, overseeing everything. He crossed the lounge and walked along a short corridor to an oversized, ostentatious bedroom. It had been deemed large and lavish enough to house the collection. He heard a fusion of voices as he approached, men and women trying to get their jobs done.

It's okay. We have tonight, Friday and even Saturday morning to finish before the big event.

Everything had to be ready for Saturday afternoon. The cameras would roll at 6 p.m. Once the unveiling was complete, the display would remain in situ for one week, whereupon it would be visited by some well-known and wealthy figures that had helped him in his quest.

His quest to bring something special to the world—to exhibit the best spectacle, the largest collection, the most incredible array of Fabergé eggs ever assembled.

With a secret.

The main event wasn't the fifteen eggs he'd managed to buy over the last decade. It was the four lost eggs he'd found.

Singh felt a rush of pride. On Saturday night the world would see something that had been lost for over one hundred years. Something it had never expected to see again.

He crossed over to the casino owner.

"Mr. Martel. Thank you for accommodating me."

"It's a historical milestone, Mr. Singh. The Azure is proud to be part of it."

"Well, I'm still grateful. I understand my requests were somewhat challenging."

"And that is our forte. Fulfilling the desires of our clients."

Singh drifted away, spying the head of security standing over by the window. The man looked harassed.

"Is everything okay, Mr. Coulson?"

"As well as can be, sir."

Coulson was known for his blunt, straight-talking attitude. He was also known as a world-class security expert.

"Is there a problem?"

"There are many, sir. Fifteen to start—all those famous eggs. Then four more—the lost eggs. And then one more—you."

"Me?" Singh was startled.

"You don't think you're a target? You are."

Singh made the mistake of looking left and right, an act which made Coulson chuckle.

"Sorry, sir, they won't be that obvious. If they come, you won't see them."

"Well, I certainly hope you can keep us safe, Mr. Coulson. And by that I mean the eggs, and me."

Singh turned away. His eggs were being unboxed with great care. It was one of the proudest moments of his life.

I can't wait for Saturday, he thought. *My dream fulfilled. What more could I ask for?*

CHAPTER TEN

It was Friday morning. Drake sat with Alicia and his team in the foyer of a huge, nondescript hotel somewhere in Middle America.

When they'd arrived, Alicia had let out a bloodcurdling shriek. "What? Are you kidding me? No way am I staying in this bloody place!"

Drake was used to her occasional protests, but they usually involved insects, Japanese Ninjas or French assassins. He saw nothing like that out of the car window.

"What the bloody hell is it now?"

"You don't see it? It's the bloody Shining hotel. Let me out right now."

Drake stared at the bleak, looming hotel ahead and had to admit she had a point. Still, they couldn't turn around now.

"Pretty sure the Shining hotel was in Colorado."

"Well, where the hell are we then?"

"Utah."

"Fuck off, Drakey. No way is that a real place."

"Just trust me, Alicia."

"Oh, sure. The last time I trusted you—when you took me out to dinner in London—we ended up destroying the poor Hard Rock Café and half of America's Parisian embassy."

"That may be true, but it won't happen again."

"Really?"

Alicia accompanied him into the hotel against her will, but soon lightened up when they got to meet their old friends again. Drake was glad to see Hayden and Kinimaka,

Mai and Luther, Kenzie and Dallas. He was pleased that Karin and Dino were along.

Most of all he was happy to see Torsten Dahl, although the two men shared little more than a gruff greeting.

"Didn't think you'd make it, mate," he offered.

"You know GPS was one of my many specialties for the Swedish Special Forces," Dahl growled.

"Oh aye, that's why I'm shocked you made it."

Dahl clapped him a little too hard on the back. Drake shook it off, trying to hide a smile. Hayden directed them to the lobby where a buffet was laid out; the entire area cordoned off.

"I didn't want to be disturbed," Hayden said with a smile. "Our first time together for over three months."

"Don't worry about that," Alicia said, staring around. "I think the axe murderer got all the other guests."

Hayden frowned.

Drake waved it off. "Ignore her," he said. "She's being paranoid."

"That's what all victims say." Alicia sat down in a leather armchair, back to the window, facing the width of the lobby.

Kinimaka sat next to her. "You're thinking what I'm thinking, aren't you?"

"Shining?"

"Shining."

Drake and Hayden rubbed their eyes at the same time, both feeling bemused. Karin reintroduced Dino, not that she needed to, and Kenzie decided to re-establish Dallas's credentials. Molokai arrived last, dusting his robes off and placing them over the back of a chair.

"Wow," Karin said. "How's everyone been?"

Twenty minutes of chatter followed. Everyone except Dahl and Molokai spoke up, but no one felt they had to.

They learned about each other's exploits in various parts of the world, about Kenzie's new role and Drake's previously unrealized jet-skiing skills.

It was a quick twenty minutes, and Drake found himself thinking he hadn't really learned anything new when it was over. Mai and Luther sat close, looking easy together, but hadn't revealed if they were a couple. Likewise with Karin and Dino. Hayden and Kinimaka were clearly together again, the big Hawaiian couldn't hide anything.

But it was Dahl they looked to when they had finished. "Sorry to hear about the divorce, mate," Drake said.

Dahl nodded, staring into space.

"If there's anything we can do . . ." Hayden let the sentence hang. Drake was sure the Swede would take the offer on board but would handle the situation himself. He wasn't the kind of man to ask for help.

"They're still in DC," Dahl said after a minute. "It's not so bad. Johanna's looking for a new place in Stockholm."

He didn't have to say anymore. Your wife moving away was one thing, but if she took the

children too . . .

Drake noticed Kenzie watching Dahl, saying nothing. He wondered what was going on in the Israeli's mind. He wondered if Dahl might end up fighting alongside her in Egypt.

Two waiters appeared and proceeded to carry several trays to the table. It was hot food. There was another half hour of idle chit-chat and eating.

"I visited Lauren and Smyth's graves a few days ago," Dahl said. "Took some flowers for Lauren. A medal for Smyth they sent from home. Tidied up a bit. Explained what we were up to now." He nodded to himself, saying no more.

Drake coughed to hide a surge of emotion. Everyone had visited the graves at some point during the last three months. It was a different experience for them all.

"How's Yorgi?" Alicia tried to keep it upbeat after a long silence.

"Finally spoke to him yesterday," Hayden said. "He hasn't called in a while because he's been feeling down. He wanted to join us. The hospital recommended otherwise, and I had to go with their advice. A shame, really, as he could be useful for this job."

Drake raised an eyebrow as everyone sat forward.

"What job?"

"But first, I have to ask . . ." Dahl said. "Why did you pass up all the other jobs?"

Hayden looked surprised. "Because you all needed some time away."

Dahl grimaced. Drake and Alicia shook their heads. Molokai looked ready to protest, but Hayden cut right across all of them.

"Don't give me your bullshit. Your army waffle. If you don't know that you needed rest. If you don't know that you needed to take at least two months out then there's something seriously wrong with you. We've been fighting for four years. Did you know that? Since Odin. There's been barely any downtime in between. We can't keep doing that and hope to stay sane, let alone alive."

"Yeah," Kinimaka said as she took a breath. "Deal with it."

His light-hearted words cut across any sharpness Hayden's tone may have held. It made Dahl smile and Drake grin. It made Alicia snort. Hayden found she didn't have to continue as the team shook any discontent off.

"And before we get into the meat of it," Hayden said. "I

have to say this. Despite the efforts of hundreds of men and women all over the world, there have been no sightings of either the Blood King or the Devil. It's known that the Devil was last seen in America, where he threatened Johanna—" she nodded at Dahl "—and it's assumed he's still there. Somewhere. Some of the mercs we rounded up after Devil's Island spoke of a plan to rebuild his domain somewhere in the US. They said he'd been developing it a while. But, whatever he's doing, he's doing it very quietly."

"That's his forte," Drake said. "It's why he's the world's most terrible contract killer. He plans and waits before he acts. It won't take him long to get set up."

"No, well, I'm sure we'll hear something. Now, as for the Blood King . . . Luka Kovalenko has dropped off the face of the earth. We know he has the nineteen low-yield nukes; we know their radiation signatures should be locatable. It would appear he's shielding them, probably behind lead-lined walls."

"He's been planning this too," Drake said. "We know that much. Probably as long as he was planning to kidnap the President and take us out. It's the next step that's bothering me."

Dahl grimaced. "Look internal," he said. "Both Kovalenkos have shown the same patterns. They buy or persuade government employees to do their bidding by any means possible. I'll bet there's a plan already in place for the nukes, and it's ongoing right now."

"I don't know," Hayden said. "He got hit pretty bad in Paris and London. Left with his tail between his legs. Even spent some time at Devil's Island. Like his father, his arrogance beat him just as badly as we did. He refused to see how he could lose. I think he's been rebuilding, proving he's not been weakened to all the sharks that circle his father's old empire. The nuke plan has been put on hold."

"Or . . ." Mai said. "It's for the future. Or maybe he intends to sell them one by one. My point is, we don't know."

"One thing I do like," Luther said, leaning forward. "Is that the Devil is gunning for the Blood King now. I bet old Luka's shitting himself."

Quiet laughter broke out. Alicia stretched. "I personally can't wait to meet that Russian prick again," she said. "But Hayden, how about making all our dreams come true. Tell us about the next job."

CHAPTER ELEVEN

"Right," Hayden said. "Well, I think you'll like this. There are rumors that the greatest heist of all time is about to go down in Las Vegas."

Excitement coursed through the room. Everyone sat forward in their seats. Alicia couldn't help herself, blurting out: "Is George Clooney involved?"

Drake rolled his eyes. "Just ignore her."

"I doubt he's part of the heist," Hayden played along. "But we'll be in the right place to meet a celeb."

"Perfect." Alicia nodded. "Maybe I can cross a few off my bucket list."

Drake turned to her. "Who the hell's on your—"

"Will you two shut up," Dahl broke in. "Hayden, continue."

"I thought you might like this one. It's different than usual, but don't worry. There'll be danger and probably some action if this thing goes down."

"A heist isn't exactly world threatening," Mai said. "Why us?"

"Well, the Strike Force objective isn't only to deal with world threats. It's managing conspiracies, individuals and other complications that might cause great harm. The heist alone would cause incredible shockwaves. And when the wealth gained from it hit any market, it could destabilize an economy. It has far-reaching implications."

"But it's just a rumor," Dino said.

"Everything's a rumor until it happens. You want to be on top of this or chasing its tail?"

"On top, I guess."

"Good. To be truthful the Las Vegas police are convinced something's gonna happen. It's the last thing their city needs too with the new stadium and football team opening in 2020. I wouldn't say they're panicking, but the mayor's more than alarmed."

"I'm guessing this isn't just a robbery," Drake said. "There are people more qualified than us to address that kind of thing."

"You're right. The robbery is rumored to be the work of the best heist team the world has ever known. They're called the One Percenters. In twelve years, they've done the biggest jobs, and have never been caught. Hardly even seen."

"So that's what's got everyone jumping." Alicia nodded her understanding. "They don't think they can stop it."

Hayden nodded. "Correct. And the One Percenters have become violent of late. There's a theory that they're coming apart. This could be their last ever job. And they might go out with a bang."

"My favorite expression," Alicia agreed. "Words I've lived my life by."

"What do we know?" Luther asked.

"My info comes direct from the FBI, who got it from the LVMPD. Someone has been buying special explosives and glass cutting tools. Industrial ones. Someone has been accessing plans to the Azure Casino, the sealed ones that nobody sees. These essentially show all the security protocols and procedures. One snitch overheard the name Kushner, supposedly the best thief in the world and a member of the One Percenters. The other members are a guy called Jax and two women, called Faye and Cara, and that's all we know. They've only ever been photographed once, and the prints are grainy. They never leave prints and have never left a crime scene anything but pristine."

"Honestly," Drake said, "it sounds good. I want to get back into the action. But where the hell would we even start?"

"Well, you investigate." Dahl frowned. "Don't they do that in Yorkshire?"

"Piss off, mate. I've investigated a few sarnie shops in my time, but this is hardly what we're used to."

"Ah, well," Hayden grinned, "that's where you're wrong. It's the subject of the heist that's really interesting."

She paused. Drake picked out two slices of bacon for himself, much to Dahl's amusement. "Diet?" the Swede asked.

"Well, three months of R&R isn't great for the figure."

"Tell me about it." Kinimaka patted his belly.

Hayden continued, "A collector, called Mr. Singh, is bringing his incredible collection of Fabergé eggs to Las Vegas, to the Azure hotel and casino in particular. Apparently, he has fifteen to show, which is the largest amount ever assembled, but he also has four of the lost seven eggs that he will reveal for the first time on Saturday. That's tomorrow. It's the biggest event on the planet right now. I'm sure you've heard of the Fabergé eggs?"

"They don't do it for me," Alicia said. "I prefer a Crème egg."

Mai tutted at her, but it was Kenzie that spoke up. "Are you kidding? Where's your respect? The Fabergé eggs are one of the world's greatest wonders."

Alicia turned to Drake. "Is the relic smuggler really talking to me about respect?"

Drake skirted the issue. "Worth a fortune I would imagine."

"Many millions," Hayden said. "The lost ones will be

priceless, although I'm sure some collector will already have put a price on them."

"This Singh guy. What do we know about him?" Luther asked.

"Self-made billionaire. Likes relics, mysteries. That kind of thing. Made it his life's goal to collect and find as many eggs as he could."

"Is there a way we can put a number on their worth?" Drake asked.

"Well, in 2007 a clock named by Christie's Auction House as the Rothschild egg sold for around nine million dollars, setting three records. It became the world's most expensive timepiece, Russian object and Fabergé egg ever sold. That's one egg, twelve years ago. That's how valuable, venerated and well-regarded they are. Singh has more eggs than the Kremlin and the royal family combined."

"And the four lost eggs?" Mai asked. "Where are they?"

"Oh, the same exhibition," Hayden said. "They're holding back the reveal until the end of the show."

"So exactly when the hell are these One Percenters gonna steal them?" Luther asked, looking perplexed. "On live TV? That'd definitely be the best heist ever."

"After the show's finished, Singh and the Azure plan to exhibit the eggs for one week. Special dignitaries, celebs and high-rollers have been invited to view them. You know the score. Mostly, it's about publicity and one-upmanship."

"Not for Singh by the sounds of it," Mai said. "It's a passion for him."

"Yes." Hayden nodded. "But anyone that wants to share their passion must in some way compromise it."

"Do we have a list of the eggs? And the lost ones?" Mai asked.

"Sure. I'll hand all the info out at the end."

"Do we have any leads?" Dahl asked. "Anything to follow up?"

"We can case the whole area, see if anything pops. Then there's the snitches to talk to. The explosive and glass cutter suppliers. We have some work to do."

"Haven't been to Vegas for a while," Drake said a little wistfully. "I remember, it used to be Kennedy's favorite place."

"Caesar's wasn't it?" Hayden asked.

"Yeah, she loved the whole concept. From the décor to the best buffet to the rooms and the Forum Shops. She could last a week without using an exit door."

Hayden nodded. "I remember her using those words as if it were yesterday. Let's not let her down."

"So we're going to Vegas?" Dino asked, unable to hide his excitement.

"We are," Hayden said. "And I don't care what that city's seen before. It's never seen anything like Strike Force One."

CHAPTER TWELVE

Las Vegas: A shimmering jewel in the middle of the Mojave Desert. A resort destination known for gambling, world-class dining, fabulous entertainment, and mega billion-dollar hotels. Known for its knack of constant reinvention, of not being scared to implode the past and build anew. To some it was simply Sin City. Others only knew it from television shows and blockbuster movies.

 Drake knew from previous research that the valley in which Las Vegas stood was found by a young scout in 1829. It featured wild, plentiful grasslands and spring waters much needed by travelers. In 1844 a man named John C Fremont arrived and wrote extensively about the area, luring others to its verdant climes. Downtown Fremont Street was later named after him. The city was founded in 1905 but it wasn't until 1931, when Nevada legalized casino gambling and reduced divorce requirements to six weeks, that the city began to flourish. Around that time the Hoover Dam was built, bringing an influx of construction workers and their families.

 After World War II, lavish hotels, casinos and celebrity entertainment started to be identified with Las Vegas and, in 1950 the Moulin Rouge, its first integrated casino-hotel was opened. From Frank Sinatra to Elvis Presley, Siegfried and Roy and Celine Dion, the stars helped the city become the greatest entertainment venue in the world.

 Drake noted the time: 1 p.m. on Friday afternoon. He was seated in the back seat of a big SUV, bored after negotiating miles of sand-strewn, straight roads. But it got him every single time—the first view of Vegas. Whether he was in a plane coming over the mountains or sitting inside a car motoring through the valley, he found himself sitting up, craning his neck, looking for the landmarks he would recognize.

The golden walls of Mandalay Bay stood ahead and to the left. The iconic *Welcome to Las Vegas* sign, created in 1959, rose in the center of the road, surrounded by tourists. The roads were busy and the sidewalks busier. Stop lights kept them immobile for what seemed like a quarter of an hour. The intersections were enormous, with bridges overhead allowing pedestrians an easy crossing, fed by escalators. Kinimaka was driving, keeping it steady.

"Seriously hope we're gonna get some downtime here," Luther said, staring at the casinos.

"Me too," Dino said.

Alicia regarded them both. "Bit of a whizz are you?" she asked. "What's your poison? Roulette? Blackjack?"

"Slots," Luther said. "There's never been a slot I can't charm some money out of."

Alicia raised an eyebrow at Mai. "Unlikely, but good luck with that."

"Never been before," Dino said, "but want to."

"Shit." Karin glared at him. "You lived in friggin' LA, and you've never been to Vegas? You don't deserve to live in California."

"It was a question of funds," Dino said, "rather than desire. Dad was so poor he used to steal us our dinner and went without himself. Mum couldn't work. Mental health issues. Asshole council wouldn't pay out for her, kept finding ways to get around it. Saved themselves around ten grand per year, then spent a million on road-widening schemes that didn't work, or bike lanes. Anyway, my brother and I couldn't even buy candy. The first day I had money in my pocket was when I left home."

"I . . . I'm . . . why the hell didn't you tell me that before?" Karin asked.

"It's not something I'm proud of."

"It's not anything to be ashamed of either. How are your family now?"

Dino didn't say anything for a while, just stared out the window as Kinimaka turned onto East Harmon.

"Dad's in prison. Serving a stretch for robbery. Brother's a car mechanic, or so he says. My mum died before I left home."

"Shit." Karin put an arm around him. Kinimaka pulled up to the curb in front of the Azure. Drake got his first close look at the casino. It rose several hundred feet straight up and was clad in reflective black panels inlaid with gold tracery. The gold glittered and glowed; the walls reflected everything. The name at the very top shone so bright it looked like it was on fire, shimmering even in the daylight. Kinimaka spied an underground parking garage and set off once more.

Ten minutes later they were outside, walking to the Azure, surrounded by an intense dry heat. Vegas was a loud and busy city; their senses were assaulted from all directions. Drake let it wash over him, attempting to grow accustomed to it, but just as he was starting to adapt, they entered the Azure's lobby.

Inside, it was blissfully cool and noticeably darker, the instant shade acting like a balm to their straining eyes. Drake's first thought was *this is a nice place to be.* The dark-gold-colored reception desk wrapped around a wall straight ahead, about eighty feet away, the focal point of the spacious, airy lobby. The group proceeded across.

"I feel naked," Alicia said.

Mai whipped her head around. "Are you trying to scare me?"

"No weapons," the Englishwoman said, patting her clothes. "Doesn't feel right."

"I agree with you there," Luther said. "Doesn't matter where I am. A bazooka strapped to my chest always puts me at ease."

Drake stayed quiet, sharing similar thoughts and knowing everyone else did too. The oddest thing was, it felt strange that they were walking into a hotel rather than walking into danger.

It took a half hour to find the right person and be shown up to the Azure's penthouse level. Their elevator, although situated among seven others, traveled only to the penthouse with no stops and needed a special keycard to access.

The doors slid open without a sound. They exited and walked along a plush corridor toward a set of high, imposing doors. Two cops stood outside.

"ID?"

"We've just gone through all this." Hayden sighed. "We're here to see Lieutenant Delmar."

One of the cops stepped aside. "Go ahead."

The penthouse suite was impressive, as Drake had expected. Lavish fittings complemented luxury furnishings and floor to ceiling windows that offered a stunning view. Drake thought he could spend hours just standing there, day and night, drinking it all in.

Delmar met them near the center of the room before an ostentatious leather sofa that could have comfortably seated twelve.

"It's been a long couple of days," he started. "I don't mean to be rude but who the hell are you people?"

Hayden showed him her ID a second before everyone

reached for theirs. Drake felt disappointed and knew Alicia would too. Their new IDs were rather special and even bore the name Strike Force.

"Ah, I remember." Delmar nodded, scratching his unshaven chin. "Specialists, aren't you? What do you know that the police department, the FBI and some of the best security consultants in Vegas don't?"

Hayden smiled politely. "Probably nothing, but we were asked to attend and some of us have come a long way. How about a little cooperation?"

"Hey, have at it." Delmar waved at the rest of the suite. "I'm too beat to argue."

The FBI were next, two suits giving them the once over, testing and fishing, trying to find out exactly who they were and if they had agendas. Hayden and Kinimaka fielded the mini-interrogation like seasoned pros whilst Drake and the others wandered around the suite, taking in the sights and the décor.

Eventually, they were allowed into what everyone was calling the Fabergé Room.

Drake stopped immediately, seeing at least a dozen priceless eggs seated atop display stands around the room.

"Whoa," he said. "No offence but should Mano really be in here?"

The big Hawaiian was already hugging an outer wall. "No worries," he said. "I'll wait here."

Drake took it all in. The room itself was wide and high-ceilinged, curved at the far end where a picture window looked out across the city. It had been divested of all furnishings so that the eggs could be displayed on their stands under special lights. Drake noticed plenty of diaphanous netting and richly colored curtains draped around so that the TV audience would see only what the producers wanted them too.

Hayden approached an older dark-skinned man who was regarding proceedings with a skeptical expression on his face.

"Mr. Singh?"

"Yes, yes. Are you the insurers?"

"Ah, no. We're . . . security consultants, sir."

"More? Well, the more the merrier it seems. How can I help?"

Hayden looked around. "I agree there appears to be a lot of security here, sir, but who's actually in charge?"

Hayden and Kinimaka walked off to talk to the man Singh indicated. Drake, Alicia and Mai hung around the older man, staring at the eggs.

"I have to say," Alicia said. "I've seen Aztec gold. I've seen pirate gold. I've even seen the bones of Odin and Thor and all the treasures that were buried with them. But these eggs . . . they're something else."

"They captured my heart twelve years ago. Captured it faster than any woman I've ever known. They're enchanting, I think."

"And they don't talk back," Drake put in with a sideways glance at Alicia.

"That's true also. I want to share them with the world, but I have big reservations."

"Oh?" Mai asked. "Why?"

"I guess I'm an introvert these days. I can't stand these grand shows. I'd prefer to be tucked up at home with a tub of ice cream watching a movie."

Mai indicated the eggs. "And the four that aren't here?"

"The lost eggs are still being prepared—" Singh nodded to his left "—in there."

Drake saw an open door that led to yet another room. Hayden and the others returned.

"Let's take a look around," Hayden said.

Drake split off with Alicia and Mai, heading straight for the far picture window. They didn't expect to see signs of interference or surveillance and weren't surprised. As they nosed around, the room emptied out a little, leaving them more space. Hayden eventually wandered over to them.

"It's secure," she said. "We're forty-three floors high. Bulletproof glass. Top-notch security. They're physical bodyguards here. Even the corridor outside is alarmed. The elevator is guarded. There's more CCTV in this room than the entire Travelodge group. I don't see what else we can do."

"Investigate," Dahl said. "You mentioned some leads."

Drake saw the Swede was keen to get involved. Probably to distract himself from personal issues. He spoke up: "Great idea. What's first?"

"The roof," Molokai said. "Clearly."

Outside, they were again in direct sunlight, squinting hard and trying to ignore the intense brightness. It was hot on the roof, and surprisingly quiet, as if they'd somehow become isolated from the world. The roof area was a vast, spartan concrete space, dotted by several anonymous light-gray units. It overlooked all the other nearby roofs bar one that was over five hundred feet away, answering Molokai's question as to whether anyone could access it from above.

"Not unless they're aboard a chopper," Kinimaka said. "Which would be seen and heard."

Drake walked with Hayden and Dahl, committing nearby buildings and landmarks to memory. Of course, any criminal outfit as talented as the One Percenters wouldn't leave signs of their passing, but it helped to know the layout of the land.

Back inside, Hayden headed straight for their FBI liaison, a woman who insisted on being called Vandie, and the bureau's crack robbery expert for Nevada.

"You may be surprised to know there are few major and genuine threats to casinos in Las Vegas," she said. "There aren't many teams across the world good enough to even consider it. The casinos are highly conscientious about employing the latest and best security systems."

"Can you tell us about the rumors regarding the One Percenters?" Hayden asked.

"Yeah, a local street gang started it. A large outfit, violent, hard to approach. Local cops got very little out of them. Most of it from a snitch they don't want to expose." Vandie shrugged. "You get it, I'm sure. The snitch is worth more to them over two years than preventing the unlikely robbery of a rich man's egg collection. You can approach them if you like, although I don't recommend it. They'd all be perfect candidates for Arkham Asylum if it was a real friggin' place."

Dahl was smiling when Drake looked over.

"Sounds like just the warm up we need." The Swede grinned.

Drake tried not to grin back.

CHAPTER THIRTEEN

Alicia stayed low, despite the overarching darkness of the night. They were approaching the ruins of a large mansion on the edge of town. She could see the remains of walls, roofs, outhouses, a play area, a dry swimming pool, several dilapidated garages and more. Broken glass lay everywhere, just scattered across the ground. Brown grass and dying trees made up the garden, illuminated by flickering torches. An array of dim lights glimmered inside the walls of the house.

Shouts, laughter and bouts of wild cheering surged sporadically from several directions: the pit of the pool, the gardens, the shell of the house.

"Impossible to say how many," Dahl said, using their comms system. "But I guess at least fifty."

"Weapons ready," Hayden said.

"Ready."

Alicia crouched, muscles coiled. Now that they were back at it, about to engage, it felt a little odd. Three months away from the edge of combat was an awful long time. It was certain that she was less sharp. Her gun, a basic Glock, felt familiar and at the same time strange, like an old friend long missed.

Did I grow used to the rest? Did I like it?

She wanted to say no but the truth was complicated. She'd enjoyed some of it, but missed much more. Most of all, she'd missed being a part of a team.

A family.

That was the right word. Alicia never had a tight-knit, loving family. Never came close. SPEAR and now Strike

Force One was everything that kept her sane.

She reviewed their Intel. The gang's leader was a man named Eastwood. His deputies were Sparky and Wisner. He also had a bodyguard called Zion. The trick was finding any of these people before bullets started flying.

To that end, Hayden had placed the overeager Dahl, Luther and Molokai at the back, hoping to minimize confrontation. Their main objective was to talk to this gang, to learn what they knew and maybe draw out a little more than they'd told the cops.

Ahead, the ruins waited; the gang screamed or shouted in anger. The atmosphere was rough, violent.

Alicia tapped Drake on the head. "You ready?"

"Well it beats the bloody Caribbean, love."

He ran ahead, keeping his head down, refraining from drawing his weapon. Alicia tracked him, Hayden to her right. They approached an outer wall, sliding into its shadow close to where half of it had crumbled. Members of the gang were close now. Alicia could hear them talking in low tones.

Hayden stepped out and raised her voice: "Police. We're here to talk to your leader!"

Alicia rolled her eyes. "Christ, she thinks she's talking to the fucking Martians."

Announcing themselves as police ensured they wouldn't be fired on, at least for now, and that they would be taken to Eastwood. It seemed the best plan. Alicia readied herself nevertheless as people rose in all directions.

"Fuckin' zombies," she said.

And many of them fit the bill. Drake was nodding along at her description as bodies rose from the pool and heads popped up over broken down walls. Figures emerged out of the garden and from behind tree trunks, all staring, all weighing up the newcomers. The subdued light didn't help, casting shadows everywhere.

"Eastwood," Hayden shouted. "We need to speak to him."

Alicia and Drake flanked her, with Kinimaka behind. Their hands hovered close to their weapons but didn't touch. A group of about fifteen individuals gathered, staring curiously or severely, some twirling knives and flexing chest muscles. Others brazenly stood with guns held loosely in one hand. After about twenty seconds of tense silence a figure jumped over a low, battered wall and approached.

"You're not cops."

Eastwood was spookily tall. Alicia thought he'd have made a good voodoo priest. Tall and thin, walking with a lurch. All he needed was a tub of white face paint.

Hayden held up one hand before plucking her ID from an inside pocket. As Eastwood approached, she handed it to one of the man's lackeys.

Eastwood took it. Alicia was fascinated by the length of his fingers which wrapped around the leather wallet before flapping it open.

"Agent Jaye," he read aloud. "With the . . . Strike Force. What the hell is that?"

Alicia winced. They'd never had much luck with IDs. Either nobody had ever heard of them or they just didn't sound right when spoken aloud.

"It's official. Agent Vandie will vouch for us."

"Vandie?" Eastwood glanced up from the wallet. "This about those thieves?"

"That's right. We'd like to ask you some questions."

"Already spoke to cops. Real ones."

Hayden took a breath. "What do we look like to you?"

Eastwood took a hard look. "Special ops. You got that

look. Ex-military. Hard cases. Damn, you probably come here for a fight."

Alicia re-evaluated her opinion of the gang's leader. "He's pretty close to the mark."

Eastwood looked at her. "Why the hell's Five-O sending out spec ops?"

"They're pretty serious about catching these guys."

"It's just a robbery."

Alicia shook her head. "Nope. It's a fucking big heist. If they pull it off, heads will roll, and one might be yours."

Eastwood eyed her. "Like I said, we've already been questioned."

Alicia glanced from eye to eye, face to face. Which one in this large gathering was the mole? Did they know more than what they were saying? It was impossible to know.

"Like you said," Drake spoke up. "We're not cops. Give us a chance."

"It's weird," Eastwood said. "But you can come through if you fight."

Alicia frowned. Hayden held up a palm. "Wait, what?"

"We're a fighting gang. Not a criminal gang. Against each other we fight for turf, the best spots to sleep. Against other gangs we fight for honor and land. Didn't Vandie tell you?"

"She must have forgotten to mention it. Don't tell me she fights you?"

"Once—" Eastwood nodded "—to earn our respect."

A silence fell. Eastwood regarded them speculatively. Hayden turned to look at Drake, who sighed at Alicia. From behind there came happy rumblings from Dahl and Luther.

"One man, one woman," Eastwood said. "We have joint champions."

Another few moments passed. Suddenly Alicia was done with standing still, with inactivity, and stepped forward.

"I'll fight," she said. "Show me the bloody ring."

The first man to her side was Torsten Dahl—as she'd expected.

"Ditto," he said.

Alicia faced a woman who wore very little apart from a six-pack, a glare and a nasty attitude. Her shorts and sports top were barely there. Alicia stripped off her jacket and her weaponry, even the short knife nestled inside her boot. There were rules.

Apparently.

Alicia didn't trust these people one bit. They marked out a circle in the ground, planted flickering torches around it, and shoved her into the middle. A crowd gathered. She could see Drake opposite, looking nonplussed and unsure. Nobody had expected this turn of events, but gathering information took precedence.

She waited, stretching her muscles. The woman she faced was called Rosa. She looked fit, strong and experienced in battle, but Alicia wondered if she'd ever fought for her life against hundreds of mercenaries, down in the dirt, exhausted and bloody, battling all odds to help save the world.

Doubtful.

Still, it needed ending quickly. Eastwood clapped twice and the battle commenced.

Alicia padded over the springy grass, closing the gap.

Rosa struck fast and hard, coming in with her fists.

Alicia sidestepped and dodged, watching the way her opponent moved, looking for strengths and weaknesses. She took a blow to the arm, a jab to the cheek. She'd bruise, but it didn't hurt.

Somewhere from the crowd came Kenzie's loud cry: "Come on! Hit the bitch!"

Alicia couldn't decide who Kenzie was cheering for.

Rosa darted in.

Alicia pretended to stumble.

Rosa switched stances to capitalize, but Alicia was already past her, unleashing three sharp strikes. Two knifed into Rosa's ribs and kidneys, making her gasp before she managed to spin and cover up.

After that, Rosa struck hard. Alicia respected the assault, watching carefully, taking blows where she knew it wouldn't debilitate her. The torches flickered in her eyes, their bright flames washing across Rosa's face. She feinted an attack, making Rosa raise her arms and then kicked her in the chest. Rosa fell to the floor.

Alicia looked at Eastwood.

"Gotta tap out," he said.

Suddenly, Rosa lost it. Snarling, she launched herself across the grass and struck up at Alicia. Surprise caught the blonde slow-footed and she barely had chance to twist her body to the side. Rosa struck her shoulder hard, sending her spinning.

Alicia stumbled to her knees. Rosa was on her back a second later, a muscled arm enclosing her throat. Instantly, Alicia felt the pressure and saw black spots as her air supply was closed off. There wasn't going to be much time, not judging by the grip Rosa had.

Alicia gathered her strength and jumped up, Rosa clinging to her, then threw herself backward. Rosa hit the ground hard, Alicia on top of her. The grip loosened. Alicia took advantage, squirming around, kneeling up and then delivering a volley of devastating blows. Rosa covered up, but Alicia knew where to hit and how hard.

Forty seconds passed before Rosa tapped out.

Alicia rose.

Eastwood confronted her. "A lesson for you."

She felt confused. "What?"

"Don't play with your food. Devour it."

He was right. Maybe it was the long lay-off. She couldn't imagine herself giving an opponent any kind of chance. It highlighted yet again the dangers inherent in relaxation.

Dahl strode into the arena, supremely confident. Alicia helped Rosa to her feet, then clapped her on the back. "Good fight."

"I shouldn't have lost the chokehold."

She was right. Alicia nodded. "Next time, go harder. The problem most people have, including innocent victims of muggings and such, is that when they get an opportunity to finish it—they don't finish it properly."

"And Spec Ops do."

"Damn fucking right they do."

Dahl waited, removing his jacket and staring at a pool of darkness so as not to ruin his vision. Soon, Eastwood stepped aside, and Alicia saw a big man enter the arena. He was stripped to the waist and slick with sweat. Clearly, he'd already limbered up. His face was craggy and hard-lined, his arms and chest crisscrossed with old knife wounds and fresh bruises. He sneered at the Swede and then roared, raising his arms and clenching his fists.

He was the champion of this street-fighting gang and his name was Tamor.

Dahl stood patiently. Tamor roamed the arena, shouting at the crowd, roaring to raise their bloodlust. He punched the air, pointed at Dahl and laughed.

Alicia winced.

Drake, standing beside her, leaned over. "This should be interesting."

Tamor bellowed for support. He flexed his muscles, every cord straining. Eastwood clapped twice, the signal to start. Tamor stalked forward, raising a huge arm to throw a punch at the unmoving Dahl.

The mad Swede showed no sign of covering up.

Tamor swung. The blow was hard and loud, striking Dahl across the jaw and sending his head to the right.

Alicia winced.

Tamor laughed, preparing to strike again.

Already low, Dahl delivered an uppercut using all the power of his thighs.

Tamor didn't see it coming. One second he was laughing, the next he was flying backward through the air, unconscious.

Tamor hit the ground, unmoving.

Dahl hadn't moved from his position.

A revered silence spread throughout the gardens.

Hayden turned to Eastwood. "Can we talk now?"

CHAPTER FOURTEEN

The torches were brought in closer as Eastwood, his lieutenants and some of the gang took up a position inside the crumbled walls of the mansion. They sat with their backs to the tumbled-down rocks, drinking whiskey and bourbon, and eating pizza. Alicia and the others sat among them, side-by-side with the gang, welcome at least for the next few hours.

Hayden addressed Eastwood: "We don't have much time. Anything you can tell us will be useful."

Eastwood shrugged, and waved a folded slice of pizza in his right hand. "Like I told the cops," he said around a mouthful of cheese and pepperoni. "Friend of ours—let's call him Lenny—was approached by some dude wanting to buy special chemicals. Lenny's connected, and didn't want to sell the dude the chemicals—they're bad shit. But the dude went above him, went to his boss, and forced him to make the deal. His boss called the buyer a One Percenter."

"That was his reason for making Lenny do the deal?"

"Yeah, that and the money that crossed his palms." Eastwood took another bite. "Truth was, Lenny thought the moniker one percenter meant the guy was super-rich. Didn't think until later that he might belong to this mythical heist gang."

Alicia accepted a slice of pizza for herself and a plastic cup full of whiskey. It wasn't a bad night as it turned out, eating and drinking with a street-fighting gang under the dark vault of a Nevada night. From their slightly elevated position they could see the bright lights of the Strip shining off to their left, always visible. A million pinpoints of light shimmered among the city streets. Further away, dark shadows encircled the vast valley: the uneven outlines of mountain ranges.

She sat back, remaining watchful but content to be back in the field.

"You've heard of them?" Hayden asked.

Eastwood shrugged. "Nothing concrete. They're legends, like all the friggin' gold mines around here. You don't know if they really exist and, most days, you don't really give a shit."

"What do you know about them?" Drake asked.

"The One Percenters are the best of the best. Heist kings. They've pulled off something like eight mega jobs without the cops coming close. There's five of them. They use tried and tested local networks—like Lenny—to gather materials—"

"You mentioned the liquids they bought are bad shit," Dahl said, waving away the chance of pizza. "What were they exactly?"

"Highly volatile shit," Eastwood said. "If you mix them . . ." He made the noise and gestures of a large explosion. "Oh, and this dude bought detonators as well."

Hayden frowned. "That doesn't sound like the best robbers in history," she said. "It sounds stupidly loud. Deadly."

Eastwood shrugged. "You asked. I answered."

"So we have liquid explosive and detonators," Dahl said. "That's a start."

"Lenny seems to have gotten quite chatty," Hayden said.

"Lenny's like that," Eastwood nodded. "He's a gregarious dude. Good man to have at the front of an operation."

"And did Gregarious Len find out anything else?" Kinimaka asked.

"They chatted for a while whilst the explosives were . . . brought up. This dude, called himself Steele. He was big, with close shaven hair like you." He nodded at Luther. "A slightly smaller man perhaps. He was arrogant though, thought he was the big shit and all that. Lenny got him talking about the job he wanted the explosive for."

Eastwood went quiet, looking around for more whiskey. Alicia passed him her own with a nod.

"Thanks. I'm leading you on a bit. All Lenny got from Steele was the name of a cop station but a specific one on East Clarke Avenue. They also got to talking about cars, this dude loved his all-American V8 muscle, and he started whining about having to learn the schematics of a bus. Thought it was a real laugh apparently." Eastwood shrugged.

Hayden stared at him. Alicia coughed loudly. "That's it?"

"Never said I was fucking CNN, did I?"

Alicia considered asking for Lenny's address but knew it was worthless. Eastwood wouldn't have mentioned the guy if he wasn't certain he'd be kept out of it. The truth was, this Steele guy had probably revealed a little too much to Lenny, but it was hardly incriminating or world-shattering.

"Is this the only mention of the One Percenters?" Drake asked a valid question, since they'd taken this job on the assumption that a crew perfectly capable of taking the eggs and then dropping them and their wealth on the open market was involved.

"No. The dude visited other sites, once with a blond female. Bit of a looker, they said. He told her he couldn't wait for Saturday and she got mad with him. But it's not just that. There's an underground, you know? Both online and on the streets. The heist gang has a following. Rumors pop up everywhere something shady is about to go down, something big. Occasionally—" he shrugged "—their followers are gonna get lucky."

"The One Percenters have a following?" Karin couldn't understand why. "They're nothing . . . just crooks."

"No," Eastwood said. "They're successful crooks. Everything that's successful tends to get a following, one way or another, either to help tear it down or watch it grow."

"That's a bit deep for a gang eating pizza and drinking whiskey," Alicia said.

"By that, she means she doesn't have a clue what you just said." Mai laughed.

Hayden rose, brushing her trousers down. The others followed one by one. Eastwood held her gaze.

"You really think it's the One Percenters?"

"I don't know," Hayden said. "But, whoever it is, it sounds like they're getting ready to cause a whole lot of trouble. Thanks for your help."

"That's cool. And you?" He nodded at Dahl "Anytime you wanna come back, maybe fight for us, you're welcome."

Dahl held a hand out. "One day, I just might take you up on that."

Alicia turned away to head out, wondering what the hell the Swede meant by that.

CHAPTER FIFTEEN

Hayden fought to focus. Like the others she believed the layoff, although necessary, had blunted their acuity. They weren't as sharp, single-minded and quick. It would return but felt a little debilitating right now.

"I'm headed downstairs," Kinimaka said.

She nodded at him. They'd been given a second-floor room inside the Azure and although it was one of the hotel's cheapest, it surpassed almost everything she'd ever stayed in.

"I'm still wired," she said. "Let's go."

They exited the room and wound their way around the long corridor to the elevators. The hotel was cool and sumptuous, the hallways quiet and wide, with high windows to both ends with incredible views. The elevator deposited them quickly onto the ground floor. Despite the late hour—it was after 1 a.m.—the hotel walkways were packed with guests. Hayden walked alongside Kinimaka, threading their way past two world-class restaurants, a respected buffet and the reception area. Once clear they walked along the other wing of the hotel. Statues lined the way. Thick, luxurious carpets were like cushions under their feet. The corridor curved and then opened onto an extensive casino.

Now, the noise washed over them.

From slot machines to video poker, blackjack to roulette and other table games they stared, frozen in place, mildly shocked. The casino area was bordered by a wide black fringe of carpet beyond which those under twenty-one were not allowed. Kinimaka walked ahead. Hayden waited for a moment and then followed. The big Hawaiian took a seat before one of the first slot machines he found.

"What's so good about this one?" Hayden asked, at his side.

"Not sure. I just didn't want to stand out too much."

Hayden flicked him a sideways glance. "Mano, you're seven feet wide. You're gonna stand out like a Samoan at a Weightwatchers convention."

"Thanks for that." He dug out his wallet and rifled through notes.

"Sorry. It was a joke. It's been a long day and, hell, I'm feeling it."

"Time off hurts," Mano said. "But only when you go back to work."

They heard a victory yell then, one unmistakably born of Alicia Myles. Hayden pulled Kinimaka away from the slot machine and around a bank of tables. Drake and Alicia were seated at one end of a Craps table, both with a drink in one hand. Alicia had hold of a set of dice and was madly shaking them.

"Shit, that's a scary sight," Kinimaka breathed.

"Yeah," Hayden said. "That really shrinks your balls."

Hayden hurried forward. In truth, everything had become a little surreal lately. Her new relationship with Mano had blossomed as soon as they went away together. Truly, it was all they needed. She felt as close to him now as she ever had. She worried and regretted all the time they'd lost. Whatever was in the past between them—the lows—was buried now. Forgotten. It was the present that mattered. Today, and every day after. When Smyth and Lauren were killed, the entire team had taken one huge unconscious step back. At the time they'd thought Yorgi was dead too. There'd been a shift in their viewpoints and they finally acknowledged a thought that had been worrying them all for some time.

Nobody can fight, non-stop, month after month, year after year. If they didn't die in the process, they'd have nothing, no life, at the end to show for it.

Nobody wanted to miss out on the best years of their lives. And though, looking back, most said it was when they were part of a fun-loving group, Hayden wanted to experience living with someone she loved.

Alicia caught Mano's eye.

"Wahey, big boy! Get over here and kiss this!"

She held out her hand with the dice inside it.

Kinimaka looked embarrassed. He was saved further shame by walking into the roulette table, earning him a suspicious glance from the pit boss and a sigh from the roulette croupier. Mano rubbed his hip and found a seat.

Alicia threw the dice as Hayden made her way to Drake's side.

"She's not armed, is she?"

Alicia whooped as her numbers came up. Drake grinned and turned to Hayden. "Bollocks. I never thought of that."

Alicia downed a shot of clear liquid. Counting the number of glasses lined up on the side of the table, Hayden guessed it was her fifth.

A waitress appeared with more. "They free?" Kinimaka asked.

"As long as she's playing." Drake grinned, taking one for himself.

Kinimaka joined in and so did Hayden, loosening up. There was nothing else they could do until tomorrow. Truth be told, there was little else they could do full stop. The One Percenters were such mythical creatures that even those that came across them knew nothing of them. Hayden's

belief was that the only way to catch them was in the act.
Tonight?
Shit, yes tonight. Maybe they should be in bed, trying to sleep.

But that thought brought her full circle around to the reason they'd taken a break. They all wanted a life. Room to breathe. To run. To live.

This was part of that, surely.

Drake blew on the dice this time and Alicia lost. Her answer was to cheer and sit back, giving the table to someone else. Hayden saw movement from the right and spied Mai and Luther heading their way. Trailing them, were Karin and Dino.

"Thought you two young 'uns would be hitting the nightclubs," Drake said to Dino.

"We did Planet Hollywood. Took photos along the Miracle Mile. Then crossed to the Bellagio. Now, we're back here."

"And we're working," Karin added. "Don't forget that."

Mai stared at Alicia. "You lost?"

"Just once."

"You'd be better on the slots anyway."

"Oh yeah, why's that?"

Hayden braced herself, as did Drake and Luther.

"One: I wouldn't have to look at your face. Two: it takes less brains."

"Really. And the great Ninja warrior would do better?"

"The great Ninja warrior knows it's pointless even to try."

Alicia carefully placed her glass down. Drake rose between them. Hayden, still unsure about the weapons situation, pulled Mai to the side. They ordered more drinks and, for a time, felt as if they might be normal people, conversing and laughing, happy in each other's company. Hayden couldn't remember what they talked about, but it kept them up until four in the morning.

Luther left first. "It's been a pleasure," he said. "And an absolute eye opener since meeting you all in the desert. Who'd have known where your adventures would lead me." He laughed loudly. "Not here. Not tonight. I don't know where the hell we'll end up next. And . . ." He leaned into their midst, big, bald head reflecting the bright lights. "That's good. I don't want to know, so long as we keep on going."

Hayden waited until Kinimaka was ready. Luckily, that happened before he'd had too many Hawaiian Lava Flows, although his motor functions were clearly affected even more than usual as three times in a row he lifted his drink only to get poked in the nose by a pink umbrella.

Hayden rolled her eyes at Drake. "It's gonna be a long journey back to the room."

"Aye, looks that way. Do you want a hand?"

"Nah, if he gets too heavy, I'll throw him in one of the fountains. That should perk him up."

"Speaking of perking up." Alicia raised an eyebrow at Drake. "We should get back to our room."

Drake wilted a little. "It's four in the morning, love."

"But your penis doesn't know that."

Drake's mouth moved but nothing came out. Clearly, he didn't have an answer to that. Hayden scooped up Mano and headed back the way they'd come. She made the journey without incident in the end, her mind pondering new and exciting thoughts.

Here they were, the old SPEAR team, having a laugh, some fun, and a little daring escapism on a work day. A potentially very significant work day. It was a new development and it served to give her a new enthusiasm, a fresh will.

By the time she got them back to their hotel room, Kinimaka was ready to sleep. Hayden lowered him onto the right side of their bed and crossed over to the draped window.

She opened them, looked out onto what was no doubt one of the poorest views on the Strip. The window offered the rough side of a brick wall and a partial sighting over the front of the hotel and the street outside. Cheap room, she remembered. The Azure had many more important guests than Strike Force One.

I wonder if they'll be saying that tomorrow?

CHAPTER SIXTEEN

After waking, they met in a small conference room. Breakfast was laid out on the table. Drake smelled bacon and almost drooled.

"We should familiarize ourselves with what we know about our enemy," Hayden said as they ate hot and cold food, and drank water, tea and coffee. "And with the Fabergé eggs. It could be useful."

"Not much to say about the One Percenters," Dahl said around a mouthful of toast. "This Steele might be one of their number, along with the blond woman. They're interested in a police station, a bus, and some explosives. The eggs appear to be a payday rather than a desire. We can expect high professionalism and misdirection."

"Well, we're in the right city then." Alicia laughed.

"Certainly," Dahl said seriously. "What do we know about their other heists?"

"Interesting you should say that," Kinimaka said. "I have a few details here." He plonked a small laptop on the table and started talking.

"2007," he said. "Their first assumed robbery. It was a bank, not surprisingly, close to Rodeo Drive. Ballsy for a starter. Quite high-tech. They went in after hours, so there was no violence involved. Took out the alarms, the CCTV and then a vault on a deadlock. It's still unknown exactly how, but they must have rigged something. Something homemade and very special. 2009," he went on, "they stole drug money from a police station. Came through the air vents before roping a hundred feet down, *Mission Impossible* style. They took a lot of flak for that one, which may be why they laid low until 2012 for their third mission. Race day—Nascar. Two hundred and fifty thousand spectators. Yes, the One Percenters stole 18 million that day, which marked the beginning of their real notoriety."

"Someone connected the three heists?" Dahl asked.

"Rumors on dark forums. Stories probably leaked by one or more of the less tranquil members of their gang. The fourth heist cemented their infamy. Somebody told a sheikh in Abu Dhabi that his vault would be cleared of exactly 999 gold bars within twenty-four hours. When asked, the person said the best heist team of all time would be completing their fourth mission."

"So they're not as low-key as we were lead to believe," Drake said.

Kinimaka clucked. "We have the value of hindsight. And they're not exactly shouting it from the top of the Stratosphere, are they? Anyway, heists five to eight involved a diamond center in Beverley Hills, a jade festival in Monaco and a renaissance painting in the Louvre. It was even posited at one point that they stole the Mona Lisa and that's the real reason the French museum now openly displays a fake, rather than the stated reasons."

"Wow," Kenzie said. "That's a major set of credentials."

"Better than yours," Alicia said. "Oh wait, do you even have any?"

"I guess kicking your ass could be one of them."

"What? When did that happen?"

Mai turned to Drake. "Look, my friend, you have to tell us what the hell you've done to her over the last three months. She's worse than ever."

"Worse?"

"More aggressive. Argumentative. Provocative."

"She's always been like that."

"No, no." Mai looked a little worried. "Not for a while now."

Drake frowned and took a moment to think about it. Mai was trying to say that Alicia wasn't entirely happy. He hadn't seen it. Alicia herself was staring at the table. Drake wondered if it was the inactivity.

Maybe Mai was reading too much into it.

Kinimaka wiped dust off the screen of his laptop. "And there you have it. A quick history of the One Percenters. They have a world-class hacker, that's for sure. Somebody that could probably hack NASA and the NSA without too much trouble. They have premier thieves, proper experts. And they have a man that can bring it all together, make it work cohesively. A formidable team. And these . . . some very dodgy photographs."

Kinimaka spun the laptop around. Drake leaned in with the others, taking in the blown-up, rough black-and-whites. It was clear that two of the shadowy figures were women and three were men. Two of the men were large, well-built, but there were very few facial features. The stills had been taken nine years ago.

"Where are we with the police station?" Molokai asked.

"Well, the police were already dealing with that information before we got here." Kinimaka shrugged. "There's nothing new. The station's been searched and searched again as have all buildings in the area. Its only tie to the eggs is that it's the closest station to the Azure."

"Speaking of the eggs," Karin said. "You may as well run us through them now."

Kinimaka finished a slice of toast and a sweet roll before he began. "Yeah, probably for the best. Mr. Singh purchased his eggs mostly from museums. Two, the Pelican and Peter the Great, were from Virginia. He bought two from private collectors. But the real draw here are the four lost eggs. Singh knew the Imperial Palace was ransacked after the Russian revolution, so it was safe to assume that, although the Kremlin only admitted to possessing eighteen eggs, there were probably more. Fourteen alone were sold by Stalin. Until now, the only proof we had that such things as the Royal Danish egg and the Necessaire egg existed, were old photos. This will be the largest display since the Russian Revolution in 1917."

"Out of interest," Kenzie asked. "Who is Fabergé? The man that created this legend."

"Peter Carl Fabergé was a Russian jeweler. Born in 1846 and died in 1920. He was one of the first artist-jewelers."

Drake checked the time. It was a little after ten in the morning. The big display ceremony and TV live event was due to begin in around five hours.

It's gonna be a long day.

He stared over toward Alicia.

Hope to God we don't have to deal with the bloody media.

CHAPTER SEVENTEEN

Kushner waited in darkness. *We're doing this. The ninth time. The greatest heist yet.*

Every single one of his senses was thrumming. He was hyper, and yet controlled, the supreme professional.

Which was more than he could say for the man at his side.

In Kushner's opinion, Steele was the team's weak link. Big, brash and self-opinionated, he was the only person Kushner wouldn't want to watch his back. Unfortunately, due to the necessary deployment of the team, Jax and Cara had to be situated on another, higher rooftop five hundred feet away. Faye was tucked away offsite as always.

Kushner crouched beneath the lip of the rooftop wall. He pulled on the special gripper gloves they'd acquired a few days ago and watched Steele do the same. He stepped into the special shoes, paused again.

"You don't have to watch everything I do," Steele muttered. "I'm not stupid."

Kushner didn't answer. Steele was, in fact, an idiot. He preferred fight to flight, a brawl to a distinguished withdrawal. Kushner's own morals were pretty low; witnessing violence didn't affect him one way or the other and he certainly wasn't as averse to it as Cara, but even he abhorred Steele's single-minded attitude when it came to confrontation. Kushner considered himself the best thief in the world—he'd proven it many times over the last twelve years—but paired with Steele—even he worried.

Kushner peered over the edge of the wall. He was looking away from the Strip, toward an office building that stood to the west, its roof about fifty feet higher than the Azure's.

Two red lights blinked. Jax's and Cara's signal. They were in place.

Kushner readied himself. Thinking of Jax and Cara, he too was perturbed at the recent fluctuations in Jax's character. They came at a bad time. Their leader had always earned his status through flawless thinking and impeccable supervision. Jax had appeared to have an extra sense, one that told him when a plan was tilting off its axis. He'd been their mastermind and nothing ever ruffled him. Maybe it was something to do with him being an ex-Marine, Kushner wondered. Nothing on this side of the world should be able to push his buttons considering what he'd seen and done in Afghanistan and the Middle East.

Eight times out and Kushner never saw Jax ruffled.

The man was a machine, able to hone that talent in between jobs because he lived alone. He devoted every waking moment to enhancing himself. This particular job had come through Cara—thus the blonde was looking like she wanted a bigger say in its development. Every idea she'd questioned, every step forward she'd hindered. And then, when Jax started acting more like Steele, Cara had noticed and called him out. Shit, even Faye noticed, and she was barely human. More like the computer she loved. She rarely came out from behind that thing, never left the base HQ on a job, and acted with robotic innocence most of the time.

Still, she was the absolute cream of the crop when it came to hacking.

Kushner worried about the One Percenters. Jax was the core, the glue that held them all together. If he went off the rails it would all end in disaster.

Steele was staring at him, a disdainful expression on his face. "You with us, or do you need a slap?"

Kushner acknowledged the gentle nudge. "I'm ready. Time for the drones."

Together, they opened a large suitcase and lifted out several industrial drones. Not weaponized models, they were most useful for delivering goods. Kushner and Steele spent some time setting them up and putting them into position.

Kushner then rose and took in the dark night. It was almost 'go' time. A half-moon hung in the sky, lending the rooftops a silvery glaze. To his east the Strip shone; droves of people pushed along the wide streets and sauntered between casinos. He could see the rear of many famous buildings, among them the enormous MGM Grand. Across the road from that the rollercoaster that circled New York-New York thundered down one of its many inclines. This high, a refreshing breeze caressed his lips, not quite getting through the breathable mask that concealed his features. The air smelled fresh, invigorating. His body was pumped.

Kushner took a breath, closed his eyes and stilled his inner spirit. Not even Steele disturbed him now, for he knew the best thief he'd ever seen was obtaining supreme focus.

Kushner was ready. The heist was on.

Five hundred feet in the air, he turned and flicked his infra-red flashlight five times. It was the signal. It was all down to timing now. Kushner started a stopwatch. Three minutes passed to the second. Jax and Cara, through Faye, should have raised eleven pre-planned alerts across the city, eight at various hotels and casinos. They ranged from fires to thefts and escaped prisoner sightings. That would occupy many of the police stations in the vicinity and even empty out some of the Azure's security, since the alerts were at sister hotels. But they were all low-key, not enough to trigger any citywide panic.

It was an extra redundancy Jax had built in. They didn't need it, but it helped. Jax was good with his diversions.

Kushner signaled Steele. He leapt up onto a low ledge. Looking down, there was nothing but five hundred feet of empty air. He would go first. They'd fixed a rope to a metal stanchion that was part of a barrier running around the roof. Kushner now strapped a separate roped harness around his body and through his legs. The harness would take most of his weight and allow him better movement.

Kushner picked up the rope, then turned his back to the drop and jumped off, abseiling down five feet before planting the soles of his shoes against the brick wall. Kushner had initially thought this method was old school and challenged Jax, pointing out the state-of-the-art Red Diamond descender, but Jax had argued that the descender wasn't as precise when it came to sending your body where it needed to be. The descender swung you, it made you dizzy. Abseiling did none of those things because you were in total control.

Kushner pushed off again, falling another five feet. The top of the building was in darkness, so there was no unnecessary risk at the moment. Kushner wore all black. He abseiled again, and positioned himself exactly where he wanted to be.

Jax had been right. This was the best way down. Maybe their respected leader wasn't losing it after all.

Maybe Cara was?

Kushner shook it away and took ten seconds to regain focus. So far, all was well. His feet were poised above the lip of a penthouse window, the one in deepest darkness due to several neighboring lights being out of order.

Courtesy of Faye and a modern casino's reliance on advanced technology.

Kushner descended another two feet, bringing his hands and the gripper gloves in reach of the window. It wouldn't be natural not to experience a tingle of fear as he secured the rope on the harness to keep him at the right height, placed his gloved hands on the glass and let go. Kushner held his breath. The gloves held him suspended almost five hundred feet above the ground, clinging to a pane of glass.

Now the breeze gusted, the wind whipping past his body, tugging at the rucksack he carried over his shoulders. Kushner ignored it, secured by the harness, made sure his feet were in the correct position, and shuffled his body around so that his head was facing downward. He climbed down the pane of glass, toward the ground, a handhold at a time.

Once in place, he glanced over his shoulder. Steele was watching over the top of the building. It would be his turn soon.

Kushner looked through the window an inch from his nose. Inside it was mostly dark, the only light thrown by a few dim security lights. The ceremony had gone well earlier today. Mr. Singh had shown off his fabulous collection of eggs and unveiled the four lost pieces to incredible applause and undeniable rapture. Those who knew their Fabergé eggs were in tears.

Kushner saw only a room filled with a happy future. Proceeds from the eggs would fund his lavish lifestyle for a decade.

Still, holding to the pane with his right hand, Kushner unfastened a small pocket in his black suit and pulled out the only thing inside – the glass cutting kit he'd created. It was a diamond-pointed scorer, a pair of heavy-duty running pliers, and several industrial strength suckers. Kushner knew that the Azure's all-black outer appearance had been achieved by coating the second surface windows with an optically thin layer of obsidian paint. Each glass layer was one inch thick. Gaining entry would require patience and skill. But Kushner was fine with that. He didn't work any other way.

Working efficiently, he cut through three layers of glass and then attached them to the uncut area of the outer window with the special suckers. With the displaced glass to his right, he now had clear entry to the Fabergé room.

Kushner signaled Steele with the infra-red flashlight. Steele would send that signal to Jax who would then notify Faye, who was seated patiently behind her top-notch bank of computers, waiting to take down the internal security network.

Kushner gripped the outer pane with the gloves. Hanging in the air was nothing new to him. He'd done it for the team several times before, trained both in Monument Valley and upon European buildings for this job. Up here, he'd first imagined he'd feel isolated, out of the real world. But the myriad noises that poured across his senses, rising from the busy streets below, made him feel as if he was among them.

In his head, he counted down the seconds.

Faye had required two to five minutes for this crucial part of the job. She'd been inside the hotel's security for a week now, sniffing out every option, but still needed time to make sure everything was perfect, from the placement and movement of guards to the ambient temperature inside the room. Faye would be spoofing feeds, looping CCTV cameras, messing with security measures such as infra-red lasers and pressure pads. She'd even be incapacitating defenses attached to the pedestals that held the eggs, taking each one separately until she had a whole.

Kushner counted past three minutes.

Finally, the signal was returned. This was Steele's cue to start down.

Kushner hung and watched him for the first few minutes, not fully confident until Steele had completed the trickiest part of the descent, and then balanced his shoes on the bottom part of the hole he'd cut in the glass.

Next, he jumped into the room, landing softly on the other wide of the window, crouching low in the shadows. This area was a room that the hotel had turned into an atrium, the antechamber that led to the proper Fabergé room beyond. Kushner could see it far easier now. It lay ahead, through an open door. It too, was in semi-darkness.

Steele appeared, puffing a little, sweating profusely. Kushner raised a finger to his lips. Steele gave him the middle finger. Kushner then nodded at the window and Steele fixed a thin piece of transparent plastic over the hole so that, for the short time they needed, it wouldn't be noticed.

"Ready?" Kushner whispered.

Steele nodded.

Together, they stole into the Fabergé room.

CHAPTER EIGHTEEN

Kushner ignored the magnificent treasures, preferring to see them as mere objects. There were five eggs each to collect, and then two lost eggs each. That would be enough. Kushner knew, by sight, the ones Jax and Cara wanted. He hurried through the dim room, placing a reflective strip on every pedestal that bore an egg they needed. That would help Steele. Then, they got down to work.

Kushner lifted the first egg, a small, exquisite piece of art called the Scandinavian, crafted in 1899. He slipped it into a specially made, unbreakable box and then into his backpack. Next was Nobel Ice, from 1914, and then three more, each one fitting perfectly into the small, foam-lined containers Cara had gotten made for them.

Once they had ten eggs, it was on to the special items.

Kushner listened to the room, to the dark. It was quiet up here, as it should be in the absolute dead of night. They were calling this the Fabergé Suite now. Mr. Singh was housed next door. Still, a patrol was expected, and Kushner knew both he and Steele had to be quick.

"Twenty minutes," he hissed, "and counting."

Residing on a stage at the far end of the room, behind a curtain, were the four lost eggs, resplendent on their marble pedestals and frilly cushions, surrounded by a plush leather border studded with diamonds. Kushner reached out for the first egg but then heard a cough.

It wasn't Steele.

Both men crouched and then turned. There was a figure by the door, wearing a cap which identified him as a guard. He shouldn't be there. It wasn't time. But he was, and he was there alone.

Some asshole taking selfies, Kushner thought. It happened more than you would think, even among the world's most respected security firms.

Kushner waited. Steele wasn't so shy. He crept through the display stands a step at a time, a shadow among shadows. For now, the guard was watching his own back, probably making sure he was alone.

Kushner bit his lip and clenched his fists. Steele had already made up his mind what was going to happen. Of course, when the guard entered the room properly, he would notice half the eggs were missing. Maybe Steele was justified.

The guard turned. Steele rose up with a palm strike, smashing the man under the jaw and then catching the back of his head before it connected with anything solid. The same hand that had impacted the guard's jaw then covered his mouth and nose, cutting off his air. Steele pressed hard. Kushner rose and walked over to them.

"No noise. Be quick."

He watched as Steele continued to press hard, holding the guard in place. He checked the outer room. All was quiet. With a swift movement, Steele now slipped behind the guard, encircled his throat in a choke hold, gripping hard. Within a minute the guard was sinking to the floor. Kushner stared at the ashen face.

"Fuck, he looks dead."

"So what? Just grab your eggs and let's move."

Kushner fought down a surge of ill will. There was no need for Steele to have done that. They were on schedule, slightly ahead. Steele had merely been proving something to himself, and maybe to Cara.

Kushner finished up, taking the lost eggs and strapping on his backpack. They exited the main room and walked across the antechamber, reaching the windows in less than a minute. Steele removed the plastic from the hole.

Kushner slipped the gripper gloves back on and then leapt up into the rim of the hole, holding the glass both inside and out. Then, he rolled his body outside and put both hands onto the glass. Slowly, he climbed.

It took long minutes to reach the top of the building. All the while he was thinking of Steele's recklessness and callousness and how Jax appeared to be heading in the same direction. The first part of the heist had gone seamlessly, everything flowing like a dream. But now, it would become harder. There was a long way to go.

Kushner stood up and signaled to the higher rooftop where Jax and Cara waited.

CHAPTER NINETEEN

The signal was returned in the affirmative. All was well.
Steele dropped down beside Kushner.
"What you did down there was immoral. I'm not one to whine or dwell if a man challenges us or tries to hurt us, but what you did defies logic."
"Shut the fuck up, Kush-baby. I do what I want. You, Jax and Cara think you run the show. Good ole Steele follows orders. But I get my kicks where and when the fuck I want."
"Your kicks? You enjoyed that?"
"Damn right. There's nothing like holding someone's life in your hands, having the power to let them live or die. It's better than sex."
Kushner bent lower as he worked, trying to disengage himself from the psychopath he'd never known he worked with. Why on earth were feelings running so high with this job? What had changed?
Together, Kushner and Steele strapped three eggs each to four drones and then two to one more. Five drones in total. Kushner took a remote from a lower compartment of his backpack and turned it on, firing up the first drone. Red lights flickered at the tips of its wings and at its nose. With a twist of a toggle button, Kushner made it rise into the air and then flew it upward on a direct angle toward the roof where Jax and Cara waited.
Thirty seconds later Jax took possession of the drone. Kushner fired up the second.
That way, they flew five drones, fourteen Fabergé eggs, and countless millions of dollars from the rooftop of the Azure to the rooftop of a nearby office building.

Jax used the infra-red flashlight to signal they'd received everything in good order. It had worked. Kushner felt excitement.

Now to the next phase of the plan, he thought.

But then, everything changed.

An alarm exploded into life, shrill and loud in the silence on the roof. Steele jumped two feet in the air. Kushner stared up at him.

"Their security's better than we gave it credit for. Shit."

Faye would be scrambling now, trying to cancel the alarm and cause a few distractions. Jax and Cara should already be on their way. It was no time to panic.

Kushner walked over to a pure black, incredibly strong length of stainless-steel cable that stretched from the top of their roof across to the Wyndham hotel. It was gradually angled since the Wyndham was a hundred feet lower. Kushner shrugged on a harness and fastened a pulley to the cable, which he then grabbed hold of.

"Go," Steele said.

Kushner leapt off the top of the Azure, hanging onto the pulley. It slid down the zip line, gathering speed. A loud grating noise filled Kushner's ears, drowning out the sound of the alarm. He was away from the Azure and halfway to the Wyndham in a matter of seconds, feet kicking in mid-air, hanging on grimly.

The hard rooftop came up fast. Kushner let go three feet before impact, hit and rolled. Pain flashed through his shoulder and down his spine, but he sprang up onto his feet, turned and signaled Steele.

Go.

He could see the big man's shadow. The alarms continued to grate through the air. Kushner shrugged out of the harness, ran to the edge of the roof, and gazed down at the streets below. Activity was light. There were no sirens closing in. But the heat was coming. Enough heat to close down the city. Kushner could feel it coming.

They'd prepared for it.

Steele landed hard, cursing. Kushner smiled in the darkness, rubbing his own throbbing shoulder. It would be worth the pain. He hurried over to the only door that lead off the roof.

It was keypad secured. Kushner punched in the code. He and Steele ran down the stairs, starting with two flights before racing across to a service stairwell for the other thirty or so. They were fast, but precise and careful. They breathed easily. They didn't stop.

Steele was at Kushner's back all the way, the big presence a little off-putting. Kushner would rather have Steele in front, so if he fell there was something big, soft and dumb to land on.

They hit the bottom, turned right through a white door, and trotted along a narrow hallway. Soon, it gave onto a storage room, full of bedding. Beyond that were some wide, straight hallways leading to a discreet side-exit door. Kushner again punched a number into a keypad and pushed at the door until it cracked open.

He checked the street outside.

It was quiet and dark. They were on the other side of the Wyndham, away from the Azure. Kushner pulled his backpack tighter and stepped outside. The sound of countless sirens cut through the Las Vegas night, sending a shiver down his spine.

"Doesn't matter how good you are," Steele whispered from behind. "Or how fast. Those sirens make your ass cheeks clench every time."

Kushner agreed. By his best guess, the cops were

approaching the Azure. Soon, they'd be flooding the area.

They kept to the darker streets, heading east, away from the Strip. They crossed Koval and turned left, ending up on Lana Avenue. By comparison, Lana was as quiet as a grave.

From the darkness, a figure emerged.

"Hey," Faye greeted them. "What happened in there?"

"Alarm went early." Kushner shrugged. "Wasn't my fault. My moves were perfect. Steele probably tripped something."

"No way," the big man growled. "Stop thinking you're the shit, man. I saw you primping and patting your hair when we got down from the roof." Steele shook his head. "Fucking Adonis complex."

Faye licked her lips. "We're on to Plan B. Not my favorite."

"Don't worry, it'll run like clockwork," Kushner said. "I came up with it."

They set off walking, heading back to Koval and then turning right, away from the Azure. Kushner frowned the whole way, thinking about what Steele had said. "You can't put a man down because he likes to take care of himself. I look good. I am good. What's wrong with that?"

"What's wrong . . ." Steele spat then took a deep breath. "Man, you're so vain that when Cara turned you down you went out and found a girl to date that looked just like her for spite. That's fucked up, man. That's weird shit."

Faye, as always kept out of it. Kushner assumed she wasn't with them in mind, just body. She'd be daydreaming of special algorithms or something.

"Cara is weird," Kushner bit back. "What's wrong with her anyway? Not wanting a guy like me?"

Steele just shook his head, giving up. Both he and Kushner still had their backpacks attached. They were full of special tools and needed to be stashed properly, which was where Koval came in handy. There was a Shell station near Westin with some overgrown wasteland behind that nobody ever ventured into. It was fenced off and locked for some reason even Faye couldn't fathom. It would be a good place to stash their backpacks until the heat died down.

As they approached an Arco station, a police car turned the corner, crawling along. Kushner saw a white face in the passenger seat, staring out the window at every passerby.

Shit.

They kept their heads down, but the car slowed even more. Kushner felt Steele tensing at his side.

"Stay calm."

"Fuck off, pretty boy."

Kushner pretended to talk to Faye, looking away from the cops, but when the one in the passenger seat shouted, he briefly closed his eyes. This wouldn't end well.

"Stop there," the cop said.

Kushner looked surprised, turning with wide eyes. "Hi," he said. "We're just heading to Caesar's."

The cop got out, hand on his holstered weapon. He glared at the three of them with judging eyes. Kushner didn't look away.

"Is there a problem?"

"I need you to turn around, hands up against the wall. Feet apart."

How is it possible? Kushner wondered.

"I'm doing nothing," Steele growled. "Until you give me a reason why."

The cop keyed his shoulder mic, about to call it in, when Steele unleashed one hundred kilos of pent-up rage. His fist smashed into the cop's face, sending him staggering, then another was buried into his stomach, doubling him over.

Steele plucked the officer's weapon from its holster and aimed it at the second cop, still seated in the car.

"Don't."

But the man was already reaching for his weapon. Steele didn't hesitate. He shot the cop in the arm, then pulled away and shot the first cop in the stomach.

Then he turned to Kushner and Faye. "Run."

CHAPTER TWENTY

When Drake and Alicia became aware of the citywide alerts, they left their room, deciding to wander for a while. Drake felt unsettled. Initially, both he and Dahl had wanted to camp out in the Fabergé room all night, but security bosses and insurance companies forbade it, declaring that their security measures were first-class and well within the insurers' usual range of experience.

Dahl tried to explain that criminal gangs like the One Percenters operated above most people's standard experience. He got nowhere.

They took an elevator to the penthouse suites, stepped out into the corridor and walked toward the Fabergé room.

"Over a dozen alerts," Drake said, flicking at his cellphone. "Bellagio. The Aria, Mirage and Planet Hollywood. Those are major casinos close to here."

"You need to stop walking and swiping," Alicia said. "You know the last person that bumped into me doing that almost got his cellphone shoved up his arse."

"I was finished anyway." Drake put the phone away.

"Cops are stretched," Alicia commented.

"Yeah, which raises my antenna."

"Really?" Alicia sent him a sideways glance. "I didn't know you had a thing for cops."

"Not that antenna. I meant my suspicions. Something's off."

"Thank God for that. No way am I dressing up as a policewoman for you."

Drake ignored her and used a keycard to gain access to the Fabergé room. The door clicked and they stepped through into one of the smaller living spaces. A guard was standing by the window and turned to look at them.

"All good?" Alicia asked.

"Quiet as the grave," he said.

"Where's your pal?" Drake looked left and right, knowing they worked in pairs.

"Recon. He went to check out the display a few minutes ago."

"Mind if we take a look?" Drake asked.

"Be my guest, bud."

Earlier, they'd been introduced to the night watch by the hotel security boss. A good move on his part. He wanted no mishaps. Drake headed for the corridor that led to the display room. The lighting was dim. Ahead, a faint glow emanated from the display room. There was no sound.

Alicia nudged him. "If that guard jumps out on us, I'm gonna fuck him up."

Drake stayed quiet, testing the silence with his senses. It was easy to get wound up and paranoid on a job like this. It was hours and days of waiting, doing nothing, and if all went well there was still a terrible sense of anti-climax. He'd been on comparable missions many times before, mostly in war zones.

"Gotta admit," he said as they approached the display room. "I never saw myself babysitting guards who're safeguarding eggs."

"When you put it like that—"

Alicia broke off as the entered the room. Drake drew in a sharp breath.

"Oh, bollocks," the Englishwoman breathed after a few more seconds.

Drake's field of view was captured by several display stands. Several empty display stands. At first, he couldn't accept it. Maybe Dahl was playing a joke. There was simply no way anybody could have crept in here and stolen . . .

Then he saw the guard on the floor in a far corner, lying motionless. Drake ran over to him. Alicia found the panic button, pushed it and listened to the claxon-like sound.

"This is gonna be a long night."

Drake leaned back on his haunches. "The guard's dead. Shit."

Alicia came over. "They killed the guard? Damn, that's cold."

Footsteps rushed toward them, boots slamming along the corridor. The guard they'd met came first, face ashen at the sight of his colleague and then the empty displays. In minutes, security staff piled in. Dahl and Luther came next, followed by more members of their team. Finally, the FBI forced their way in with several policemen.

"I can't believe it. I just can't—" Coulson, the head of hotel security, had been repeating the same phrase since he arrived. He turned from stand to stand and stared at the dead guard. His face was pasty white, his eyes wide.

The head FBI agent was open mouthed. "I don't get how this happened."

Drake saw another figure push its way into the room. When he looked over, he saw Mr. Singh. The billionaire collapsed with his head in his hands.

"A lot of people doing nothing here," Dahl said. "We're wasting time."

"He's right." Luther was looking for someone senior and in control. "The guard they killed only left the outer room ten minutes ago."

Several men were visibly trying to pull themselves together. Some leaned against walls, others just stared at the empty displays. Someone thought to check on the four lost eggs and returned with the grimmest look on his face. "All gone."

Singh let out a wail. Someone grabbed him by the shoulders and escorted him away. Drake rose and stepped away from the dead guard as medics appeared. He caught Dahl's eye and nodded at a corner.

Most of the team met there.

"What are we thinking?" Luther asked.

"What do we know?" Drake said. "They bought explosives, for sure. Shit, they need to check this room. They might blow it to cause a distraction."

Alicia darted off, followed by Mai and Molokai. Drake heard them calling for attention and laying out the possibility that the room might be wired. Immediately, everyone checked the room and someone called the bomb squad.

Drake walked across to the window. "No way they got in here. It's solid."

"There are other rooms off the corridor," Dahl said.

Two minutes later they stood before a large window with a hole in its middle. A hole large enough to admit a man. To the left of the hole, the pieces of glass that had been removed were attached to the outside by heavy-duty suction pads.

"The roof," Dahl said. "Now!"

They moved fast, explaining to the FBI as they went. Drake removed his handgun and held it close. They found a stairwell, followed it up to a door, then entered a code. Soon, they were outside in the cool night air.

Drake and Mai rushed to the right, toward the Strip, finding nothing. Dahl and the rest went the other way and called out when they found the abseiling rope and zip line.

"They're gone," an FBI agent said. "Alert the police. Do we have CCTV footage?"

Finally, someone wanted to take charge. Drake then heard a conversation between him and a colleague, stating that the insurers had insisted some of the cameras fitted inside the display room were old-school, not connected to Bluetooth or W-Fi signals. Apparently, it was a popular thing to do these days. Progress, especially electronic, would always be intensely vulnerable.

"Yes, sir. We have a few captures," the lead FBI agent was told. "Two men, one skinny, one well-built, wearing black suits and carrying black backpacks. They have facemasks on, sir."

"Never mind. Get the general description out right away. They can't be far. And get some units over to that hotel."

He pointed at the Wyndham, where the zip line led.

Drake listened as a citywide manhunt was ordered. Standing there listening, he felt superfluous. Not entirely sure what to do, he gestured at the rest of the team. "Wanna check out the Wyndham?"

"They killed a man." Dahl nodded. "That makes this personal."

"We couldn't prevent this," Hayden said. "We couldn't have known."

"Clearly it's been a long-term plan," Dino said, scratching his head. "But where would they go next?"

Drake narrowed his eyes at the half-Italian. He was right. If the One Percenters had left this rooftop, say even five minutes ago, they'd be exiting the Wyndham by now, if not further away. The real question was—where were they heading?

Hayden looked out across the city. "If their plan's long-term, they have an outlet. Several probably. They knew this might happen. And they're not afraid of murder."

"They don't know we have them on camera," Karin said.

"Doesn't help," Hayden said. "Once they're away they'll change clothes and lose the backpacks. We won't know them from anyone else on the street."

"Wait." Luther turned to them, his bald head catching the faint light of the moon. "How about the other information we have? The police station and the bus."

Drake wondered how it fit together. "I can't imagine how the police station fits, but the bus might."

"For a getaway?" Hayden asked. "It's pretty mundane."

"Exactly," Drake said. "It's understated. Discreet. It's bloody perfect. The backpacks will fit right in too."

"You want us to check out every bus station in Las Vegas?" the FBI man had been listening. "On a hunch? If you're wrong, we'd lose all momentum."

"How many bus stations are there?" Hayden asked.

"You kidding? Dozens. And there's the operators too. Greyhound. Megabus. Amtrak." He shrugged. "Too many."

"But . . ." Dahl said. "Using the bus makes sense. The stations run twenty-four hours a day. Buses leave every minute. And then there are the events, conventions, functions, parties. You'd be best served to do whatever you can."

The agent stared between Dahl, Hayden and Drake. "Who the hell are you people again?"

"You know who we are," Alicia answered with a mysterious inflection in her voice.

"Get me some evidence," the FBI agent said and walked away.

Drake opened his mouth to speak, but suddenly a cry went up around the room. Everyone turned to a cop holding a radio close to his mouth.

The cop looked up.

"You won't believe this," he said. "But we've got them!"

CHAPTER TWENTY ONE

It was a huge operation, fluid and noisy, brash and aggressive.

And Strike Force were in the vanguard of it. Even as he ran from the Azure, Drake was shrugging into a flak vest, checking his Glock, getting thrown an SIG machine pistol and strapping on a new comms system. It was a fast dash, a running jumble of men and arms as the vast security machine grinded into action.

They jumped in police cars, into vans. Into anything that was getting ready to race with blue lights flashing and sirens screaming along Las Vegas Boulevard as fast as it could. They didn't have time to strap in, barely had time to take a seat. Drake was thrown backward as his car took off. Kinimaka, next to him, lost his gun and scrabbled head first in the footwell for it.

He was wedged down there for a while, so Drake shouted over the top of his broad back: "You get any more info?"

Dahl slammed a fresh mag into his Glock, looking grim. "Yeah. FBI guy said those old, crappy black and white photos were matched to a recent robbery in California. Two pairs of high-tech gloves were stolen. The kind of gloves that help you stick to a window five hundred feet in the air."

Drake slammed his Glock in its holster and brought the SIG around, resting it on the seat. "And they matched that to someone here, in Vegas?"

"They didn't wear masks in California. Sloppy. Didn't have time, I guess. Must have been a rush job. Anyway, three of them are here, yes."

"Three?" Drake leaned over Kinimaka's back to study the photos.

Kinimaka groaned. "That's not helping, guys."

"No name match," Dahl said. "Just faces."

Drake studied the three grainy photos, taken six years ago. Then he compared them to five more, taken two days ago.

"Facial rec identified them in a bar at Caesar's," Dahl said with some bemusement in his voice. "Nobody's approached them yet."

Drake felt bewildered. He didn't have to say it was one of the oddest situations they'd ever come across. If these three were part of the One Percenters, why were they sitting there so openly? Why weren't they running? And where were the bloody eggs?

"This just gets weirder and weirder," Alicia said through the comms.

Drake held on as the car swung hard right, drifting onto the Strip with sirens blazing. The traffic had been stopped. He looked through the back window, seeing the stunning sight of nine cop cars and two police vans in hot pursuit, all screaming onto Las Vegas Boulevard in a line, tires screeching.

People lined the streets, stopping and gawking. Some gave chase. The fountains of Bellagio erupted to the left, huge spouts of brightly lit water reaching to the skies. The golden Eiffel tower flashed by to the right. Cops were everywhere on the sidewalks, holding people back. The traffic signals ahead had been cordoned off. Drake saw Caesar's appearing to the left and then his car was slewing hard across the junction, crossing the other carriageway and entering the road that led to the front of the hotel. The FBI were out first followed by Drake and Dahl. Two SWAT vans were already parked up. Dozens of cops stood near the doors.

"We ready?" someone shouted.

"Ready," the SWAT commander said.

"Go!"

Drake ran with Dahl, Kinimaka and Luther just behind him. Cops and agents surrounded them. A bomb squad van screeched to a halt close by. Drake passed through the outer doors and into the hotel, blessed by a gust of cool air. Civilians were everywhere, being herded away from danger via a far door.

The SWAT crew streamed to the left. People jumped out of their way. Drake held the SIG pointed at the floor, trying to get closer to the front. Dahl was already there, loping along like an eager Labrador at the head of the pack. Drake's comms flashed with heated exchanges. Ahead, a restaurant appeared. Its staff had been told to act normally. It had been cordoned off from both ends of the corridor that led to it, so nobody could warn the suspects. Inside, all was normal.

Drake readied himself. The entire force stopped and took a breath, hidden by the curve of the corridor.

Twenty seconds passed.

"Are we go?" the SWAT commander asked.

"Go."

There was a blur of action. Men leveled their weapons and ran at the restaurant's door, kicked it open and surged inside. They shouted at everyone, at customers, staff and especially the suspects. Drake felt long moments of tension. He aimed the SIG at the table where all three members of the One Percenters sat, keeping steady and breathing easily. The suspects were made to raise their hands and then lie on the floor. Then their fingers were tested for explosive chemicals. Finally, they were hauled back into their seats.

Drake and the rest of his team moved forward, closer to

the table. Cops dispersed, herding customers and staff out of the room. They would conduct an interrogation right here and now.

"Names," the FBI team leader, a man Drake now knew was called Paulson, said.

"Where're the explosives?" Dahl asked.

Paulson shot him a hard glare. Dahl shrugged.

Drake studied their captives. One was a tall, slim man with stylish hair and a soft face. An arrogant smile played at the corners of his mouth. Another man sat next to him, a large brute with big hands clenched into fists, looking as if he wanted to smash everyone in sight. Finally, there was a small, dark-haired woman, sitting uncomfortably as if she hated company, leaning more toward the cops than her colleagues.

"We got you," Paulson said. "It'll be easier if you cooperate."

"You got us?" the tall, slim one repeated. "For what exactly? You have evidence?"

Paulson glared. "You're the One Percenters."

"I don't have any idea what that means."

"You robbed the Azure tonight."

"That would be tricky, considering we've been here since this afternoon."

Paulson sighed. Drake studied the captives. None of them looked scared or insecure. In fact, they all appeared cool and unruffled.

"Look," Paulson said. "Normally, we'd do this at the station. And that's still a possibility. But we're on a clock here, guys. Tell us where the eggs are, and it'll go easier for you. We want the explosives too."

Drake looked around. Cops and members of SWAT and the bomb squad were searching the restaurant but coming up empty-handed.

"Listen," the woman spoke up now. "Like he said, we've been here all day. Why don't you check the surveillance? This casino must have a million cameras."

Drake watched her speak. Hayden, to his right, whispered in his ear.

"She's entirely too confident. They've rigged something."

Drake nodded. Already, he was certain they wouldn't crack. He was also beginning to believe their alibis might hold up. Was this another diversion? A way of giving the other two members of their team time to escape with the eggs?

"I want to see your evidence," the arrogant one said.

Paulson turned away, conferring with fellow agents and local detectives. Soon, three men were leaving the restaurant with the hotel's manager, their instructions to find the pertinent footage and send it back.

"What's their game?" Karin asked. "This is clearly staged. They knew we had photos. They knew we'd connect them."

"Hey," Dino shrugged, "you're the brains. I'm just the muscle."

Both Luther and Molokai looked down at him. "If you're the muscle, I'm the subtle one," Luther growled.

"Plus, they're in police custody now," Hayden said. "It doesn't sound like the best plan in the world."

"No," Drake said. "Because there's something more to it."

He planted two fists on the table, leaning forward and staring the big man in the eye. "What are you three wankers up to, eh?"

The arrogant man gave him a thin, assured smile. Drake wondered if he might get a chance to wipe it clean off his face. Dahl was already thinking on similar lines, looking for Paulson.

"Two minutes," he called out to the FBI agent. "Clear the room."

Paulson squinted at him. "You wanna beat it out of them? I don't think that's gonna work, big guy."

"It's worked before," Dahl told him. "Can't hurt to try."

Paulson returned to stand before their captives. "First one of you to sing gets to walk."

A tension fell among those gathered around the table. Drake saw the first signs of disquiet among the three. *They're worried one of them's gonna speak up, which makes them far from the tight, perfect crew we thought them to be.* Watching them, Drake thought Steele might be the one he could make crack. He might be big and tough, but he was volatile too. Drake could work very well with volatile.

"No takers?" Paulson prompted them.

The arrogant one leaned forward. "My name's Kushner," he said. "This piece of meat is called Steele and that's Faye."

Again, Drake was shocked and tried not to show it. He hadn't expected this. What the fuck is going on?

"Where are the eggs?" Paulson asked.

"They're on a bus. A red-eye to Los Angeles."

Paulson stared. Drake felt a surge of conflict inside. He didn't believe it, but then . . .

"But there's a catch," Kushner said.

Dahl raised his SIG and pointed it right between the man's eyes. "There usually is."

"Don't be a dick, soldier boy. I know you're not gonna shoot me."

Dahl pressed the trigger. The bullet exploded out of the gun, passing close to Kushner's ear. Everyone in the room leapt out of their skins or dived to the floor. Paulson included.

"Are you fucking mad?" Paulson raged, climbing to his feet.

Kushner had failed to remain straight-faced. Fear twisted his features, and his chest heaved and fell.

"That smile's gone," Dahl pointed out.

"Leave!" Paulson cried. "Get out of this room. If you try to get back in, I'll have you arrested."

Dahl didn't argue. He'd known what would happen, Drake guessed. But now Kushner and the other two were far more agitated.

"You said something about a catch?" Mai asked in a sugary voice.

"Ah, yeah, yeah. The eggs are on a bus, like I said. But you're not gonna be able to retrieve them."

Paulson leaned forward. The entire room was rapt, staring at Kushner. Drake couldn't tear his eyes away from the man.

"Why?" Paulson asked.

"Because there's a bomb on that bus. When the engine starts, the bomb is engaged. If the engine is ever switched off, it will explode."

Drake couldn't believe his ears. There were gasps, cursing, cries of disbelief. Kushner had that smug smile back on his lips.

Paulson was aghast. "Are you fucking mad? Get these assholes down to the police station."

CHAPTER TWENTY TWO

Cara boarded the bus with twenty other passengers, a dozen steps ahead of Jax. Half the eggs nestled in her backpack. They'd left the drones back on the roof of the office building. It didn't matter when they were discovered.

After unstrapping the eggs from the drones and packing them away, she and Jax had made their way to street level, where they flagged down a taxi and traveled to a Greyhound bus station. They'd had to wait a short while for their connection. At this time of night, the service to LA was less frequent.

"Not good," Jax said now as he slid in alongside her near the back of the bus. "Not good at all."

"Plan B?"

"Yep, this is definitely Plan B. Maybe even fucking C. I can't believe they made the others so quickly. And those alarms went off early."

Cara nodded. "Chance," she said. "Bad luck."

"Well, chance and bad luck is gonna cause a lot of people a shitload of pain."

"Jax. Relax. We did it."

"Not yet."

"The plan worked like a dream. You saw those drones flying from the Azure with their beautiful cargo. They were stunning."

Jax smiled briefly. "The most expensive cargo in the world," he said. "Wait here." He moved to rise.

Cara placed a hand on his arm. "Do you really have to do this part?"

Jax frowned and scratched his thin stubble of hair. "You

know we do. Kushner, Steele and Faye are headed to the cop station. We'll be found by the time we reach LA. Don't worry, it'll be fine."

Cara looked into his eyes, seeing a pain there. A pain she'd never seen before. "Are you okay?"

"Look, I'm fine. Distracted is all. I'm thinking of a hundred ways this could go wrong and a hundred contingency plans." He patted her hand. "Two minutes."

Cara watched him walk down the aisle toward the driver. Her stomach clenched. She watched him engage the driver in conversation. He'd probably be using the ex-army angle. Many civilians were sympathetic to that and enjoyed having a Marine aboard their bus. Less than two minutes later, Jax was on his way back, a hand thrust into his right pocket.

"You got it?" Cara asked.

Jax briefly showed her the driver's phone. He'd distracted the man well enough to slide it out of his big jacket pocket. At that moment the bus was turned on. The engine roared.

Jax looked Cara in the eyes. "We can't stop this now."

She swallowed drily, fearful. The bus shuddered and pulled away from its berth outside the Greyhound bus station. She'd counted twenty-two other passengers, youths and old people among them. In her brain, she knew there was nothing to worry about. The bomb shouldn't ever go off. But in her soul, she worried, not least due to Jax's recent change in attitude.

Privately, she vowed to make sure everyone escaped the bus. It wasn't a great idea, but it did ensure their passage to LA. Plan Bs were never pretty, but this one was downright ugly. When they'd learned the cops had pictures of them all, and were using facial recognition, especially in Vegas, it had triggered the backup plan. Nobody liked it, but they had to fall back on it. If they didn't, they'd get caught.

She imagined the liquids mixing in the container underneath the bus. She shivered and wrapped her arms around herself. It was going to be a long drive through the night.

Backpacks nestled by their knees. She didn't want to calculate how much they were worth, not yet. All those eggs. Fabergé's life work. Singh's collection, obsession and life goal. All ripped away by the One Percenters.

But she hadn't done it for the money, or the notoriety. Cara was a consummate professional, obsessed by the artistry of the job. She'd done eight heists with this team, the greatest eight heists in history.

But this one . . . apart from the initial robbery, it was a jagged plan at best.

Why had Jax chosen it, and how had the finer details passed her by?

She knew why. The initial plan—the rooftop descent, the gripper gloves, the security hack and the drone solution were brilliant. It had captured her imagination. In fact, it had so bedazzled her that she'd not been interested in anything else. They were a great team at that point. Eight out of eight and no real issues. Why would she be interested in a Plan B?

It was only later that she realized the team wasn't what it used to be.

Sitting on this bus, being jounced away from Las Vegas, was the price she paid for complacency.

The bomb was unnecessary. It was Jax's idea, backed up by Steele and an unconcerned Faye. Supposedly, it guaranteed they wouldn't be caught and, this time out, Jax appeared to need—to crave—that ultimate guarantee.

Why is that?

Something had changed, but Jax had always been a remote leader. The man in charge you couldn't really approach. It had been his way of maintaining respect and loyalty. Now though, he was entirely withdrawn.

Cara gently tapped the bag of eggs with her boot. She stared out the window. Jax was staring at her.

"What?" she said with bitterness in her voice.

"You don't agree with this?"

"It's not us, Jax. Not how we do things. This is the end for me."

"It means we'll be free. All of us."

"It's a dumb plan."

"It's Plan B." He shrugged.

"Surely there was another option."

"There wasn't time," Jax said, pausing to think before continuing. "Everything just happened all at once. It went from planning to execution faster than any job I've ever done."

Cara watched him as he spoke. His eyes darted left, right, and to the front of the bus. "Is that really what the problem is?"

He didn't answer. He wouldn't even look at her. Cara thought about Faye, Kushner and Steele, who'd be sitting in that police station soon. They were a group of opposites who, when brought together, worked incredibly well as a unit. It wasn't a case of opposites attract, more like opposites connect. For a little while at least.

Between jobs, they never saw each other. They lived separate lives. Cara had no idea what the others did. For all she knew, they could be cops. They could be married to each other. Have children. Somehow, she doubted it though. Before today the authorities had possessed some grainy black and whites of them, taken by an informer who, later, Jax sent Steele to talk to.

She didn't want to know how that went down.

And that was the issue. She'd accepted their shit, their over-the-top antics because, together, they worked like a dream. And she loved the dream.

It was all over now.

Cara had money stashed away. Enough property and other investments to live lavishly for the rest of her life on some warm beach, far away. She could soon change her appearance. It was her only choice now. But she knew she'd always crave the opportunity to pull off one more perfect heist.

To sit down and fine-tune an already excellent plan.

"Like I said," she whispered, staring into space. "After this, I'm out."

CHAPTER TWENTY THREE

At first, even Drake was at a loss. What had started out as a heist was fast becoming a national crisis.

Paulson questioned Kushner some more, but got nothing more out of him. After that, he sent the three One Percenters to the local police station, accompanied by a plethora of men. Once they were gone, he called the most senior policemen and agents in the room to him.

"Assuming he's telling the truth, this shit just became a crisis. I want to know every bus that left this city in the last hour. It'll be a red-eye, non-stop. The important thing is to identify that bus and then contact the driver. Get some choppers in the air."

He turned to Hayden. "Get your team moving. Separate cars. If we locate all those buses quickly, we can tackle the right one when we have confirmation. It's a five-hour coach journey to LA and we might already be an hour behind, so get going."

Drake guessed there'd be several buses going to different terminals in LA. How could they find out which one had the bomb on board? His adrenalin was already up. He waited impatiently as Hayden turned to them and then thought for a minute.

"I'll stay here and help identify the bus with Mano, Molokai, Karin and Dino," she said. "The rest of you get going, and don't hang around. Find a ride. A cop car. A fast car. Anything, just catch those friggin' buses."

Drake nodded and rushed off, followed by the others. It was a crush and a mess. Cops were everywhere. So were black-suited agents, but in truth there was so much chaos any one of them could be imposters. It was the way Drake's mind worked. Never assume anything.

Soon, they were back out into the night, bathed in the bright casino lights. Statues and fountains stood to both sides and the front of the hotel was an endless procession of newly arriving cars.

Drake looked at Dahl. "That was an FBI order, right?"

Dahl was on the same wavelength. "Any car," he said. "A fast car."

Cops poured past them, heading for black-and-whites, unmarked sedans and powerful SUVs.

"A fast car would be better," Drake said. "We'd get there quicker."

"Absolutely." Dahl watched the cars as they came up the driveway. Drake was checking those parked nearby.

"What are you waiting for?" Luther barged past them. "Get a move on."

Predictably, he leapt into a big G-Wagon, pulled the driver out and flashed his ID. Mai ran around to the passenger side, caught up in the flow. Alicia found herself close to the rear door and jumped in.

Drake glanced at Dahl. "Interesting."

"Yeah, if she's not with you that kinda means you can go faster."

The G-Wagon roared away from the front of Caesar's Palace, bullying the smaller cars out of the way. In just a few seconds it had merged with the traffic on Las Vegas Boulevard.

"My ride." Dahl spied a flash of blue and started running. Drake noticed Kenzie right behind him and didn't know whether to grin or grimace. Dahl commandeered a Porsche 911 Cabriolet, following Luther's example when dealing with the driver. The Swede looked surprised when Kenzie jumped in, but didn't slow. Soon, he was burning rubber out of the drive. Drake found himself alone.

Just as he thought he was going to have to make do with a souped-up cop car there was the blip of a throaty engine and something magical arrived. Drake couldn't keep the grin off his face as he set off, stopped in front of the car and gestured at the door.

"Out."

He showed his ID and jumped behind the wheel. The badge on the steering wheel in front of him was silver, a Jaguar. The F-type sports car let out an incredibly noisy bellow as he put his foot down. For a second, the back end swung, warning him that too much use of the right foot would make him the subject of some embarrassment, but Drake caught it and then peeled away from Caesar's, joining the traffic along Las Vegas Boulevard for a short while before spying Spring Mountain Road ahead and a way onto the I15.

He swung the Jag past traffic with the iconic Treasure Island hotel standing tall and dazzling to his left, its now redundant pirate ships outside. Soon, the I15 on-ramp appeared and he powered down it, booting the engine as much as he dared. Ahead, somewhere, was Dahl and the others all racing out of Las Vegas and toward Los Angeles, any amount of buses in between. He saw helicopters above, sweeping through the skies, and the enormous construction to the right that was the new stadium.

Darkness closed in a little as he left the glitzy city behind, driving up toward the surrounding mountains and the passes in between. He checked his comms, his radio and his phone. All were working. It wasn't risky to drive harder now, since they knew the bus was a good hour ahead. It was a matter of closing the gap. Hopefully the choppers would pinpoint the bus first.

He passed two police cars at speed, saw the drivers stare at him and gave them a thumbs-up. He didn't expect to get stopped. Tonight, it was chaos.

They were all headed the same way. He passed a police van and a big cruiser. He heard them talking on their radios and answered before gunning the engine and disappearing into the dark night. He followed red tail lights, using them as guides. The road flowed onward.

An hour later the police radio crackled into life. It was Paulson, the FBI agent, with an update.

"Listen up. We've narrowed it down to eight buses. All heading for various Los Angeles locations. There are a further five close by. It could be any of them, but we're concentrating on the first eight. We're now asking the LAPD for help as those buses get nearer. I'm sending registration plates and aerial roof markings. Any of you seen a coach yet?"

Drake hadn't. He also knew it was unlikely. If a coach was traveling at sixty and you were managing up to seventy, flitting in and out of traffic, it was going to take hours to catch it up. You had a ten miles per hour advantage, maybe a little more, which would put the coaches in LA at the same time as their pursuing vehicles.

Paulson was laying down his thoughts. "We can't block the roads. We can't alert the thieves as to what we're doing, which makes helicopters risky. We can't risk the passengers unnecessarily. We're considering contacting the drivers, but even that could pose a risk. Keep driving and I'll update you again soon."

Drake expected Hayden to send the plates and the aerial marking information through, as he had no direct contact to Paulson. He called up Dahl and Luther on the cellphone.

"You guys hear all that?"

"Yeah," Luther shouted back over the roar of his engine. "We're halfway to LA and no coaches."

"Shit, you're way ahead of me." Drake pushed his gas pedal down as far as he dared.

Mai, who was riding shotgun in Luther's vehicle, jumped on the line. "Give me your registration, Drake. I have to pass our IDs and car registrations along to LAPD so they don't interfere with us."

Drake remembered and reeled it off. It was a short private plate.

"They're trying to pinpoint the coaches using their transponders," Mai said. "Hayden just called me. The issue they're struggling with is should they even try to stop the buses?"

"I really doubt the One Percenters on board will want to kill themselves," Drake said.

"But nobody knows that," Mai said. "Look at the other three. Sat waiting for us to arrest them."

"That wasn't complacency. That was planned."

"Agreed. But the FBI won't risk any civilians aboard that bus, and nobody can blame them."

"Are they contacting the drivers?"

"No decision's been made."

Drake came upon another bunch of cop cars, all with lights flashing, powering down the double-lane carriageway as fast as was reasonably safe. Steadily, he inched past them.

"You in the Jaguar—are you with the task force?"

One of the cops was challenging him. If he was with the task force he'd have a radio.

"Yes, sir. All the way."

They powered through towns that appeared out of the dark, brightly lit oases in the black night that hurt Drake's eyes for the few minutes he was blasting by. They passed gas stations and attractions. They wound through the Sierra Nevada. They negotiated roadworks near Halloran Springs and then hustled through Baker and Barstow. Drake recognized Barstow—he'd stopped there a long time ago when working for the British government to use a facilitator called Stitch, a man that paved the road on either side of the law.

The clock ticked. After Barstow they cut through more and more built-up areas. Drake took another call from Mai.

"Just a heads-up," she said. "I've been told by the guys in Vegas that the press is sniffing around. Somebody's leaked something and we don't know what."

Drake cursed. "That's just gonna complicate the balls off everything."

"Exactly. Stay frosty."

"Hey," he said, keeping his eyes on the road. "How's Alicia doing in the back seat?"

"I always thought it was her favorite place to be." Mai's voice carried an amused tone. "But she's looking a little sick."

Drake laughed and addressed his next comment to Dahl. "And Kenzie? You two okay in there?"

The Swede's voice was tight, holding in his emotion. "We're fine. Just drive."

Drake put his foot down as a passing area approached, flicking down the paddle-shift to engage lower gears. The car's headlights sliced through the night.

Somewhere ahead was a bus carrying a fortune in Fabergé eggs.

And one big-ass bomb.

Drake prayed they'd be in time.

CHAPTER TWENTY FOUR

In Caesar's, Hayden grabbed Kinimaka and rounded up the others. She spoke briefly to Paulson, grabbing a radio and exchanging numbers. She told him they'd concentrate on the explosives simply because she already had a lead.

The street-fighting gang.

Together, they found a big SUV. Karin, Dino and Molokai climbed in the back. The big man was their explosives expert, but even he couldn't advise anyone without knowing what its components were.

"Won't it be pretty standard stuff?" Dino asked as Hayden roared onto the Strip.

"You really don't wanna guess this stuff," Molokai told him, "even when there're no civilians involved. That one time you guess, that's when some asshole will have meddled with the formula. Or used an exotic constituent that changes the mix. Also, if we can determine which trigger mechanisms were used, I can advise them, which will make defusing the bomb much quicker."

They drove south, left the Strip and headed back to where they knew the gang lived. Pure, syrupy-thick tension filled the car. Hayden tried not to think about that bus and its driver, and what would happen if just one thing went wrong. An unknown factor that made him turn off the engine.

Crazy risk.

But wasn't that what these people liked? The risk? They thrived on it. Her major goal was identifying the right bus.

Soon, they approached the ruins of the mansion. Hayden parked up and drew her gun. Molokai and Kinimaka walked alongside her, big semi-automatics cradled in their arms. Karin and Dino carried an assortment of handguns.

"No messing," Hayden said. "No mercy. We're here to save lives."

Suddenly they were running, on a vital, dangerous mission for the first time in months. Hayden felt excitement, but bit her lip, forcing the feeling down. It wasn't right now, with everything that was at risk. It felt wrong.

Ahead, a figure rose up. "Hey!"

Molokai bulldozed him to the ground. Hayden heard bones crack. The man didn't get up.

They raced to the center of the ruins, where both Alicia and Dahl had fought not so long ago. Hayden fired into the air as the others leveled weapons. Bodies rose and yelled out warnings. People scrabbled for clothing and half-empty bottles, knives and guns. Hayden fired again and yelled out a warning.

"Police! Don't anyone fucking move!"

The area was lit by flitting shadows, thrown by several guttering torches. Hayden strode over to the place she remembered Eastwood sitting. Once more, she fired, this time into a stone ruin.

"Eastwood," she said. "Get your mangy ass here."

The man was already on his feet, trying to shrug his body into a pair of trousers. Hayden took out a flashlight and illuminated him, much to his embarrassment.

"Hey, hey, woman. Not fair."

"Shut it and get over here before I shoot you."

Eastwood fell to his knees, managed to pull the trousers on and shielded his eyes against the light. Hayden checked her perimeter, and saw dozens of gang members approaching.

"Seriously," she said. "This time, it's life-threatening. Stand down, all of you."

To his credit, Eastwood waved them away before fixing Hayden with a glare. "What do you want now?"

"We need to know about the bomb," she said. "First, who sold this One Percenter the chemicals and second, where does he work?"

Eastwood took it in, showing no emotion. "Something's happened?"

"Not yet."

Eastwood swallowed drily. "This guy, if he found out I told you, it'd start a war."

Hayden couldn't help but notice how his eyes flicked over his own people. Eastwood knew he had rats.

"I feel for you, but this has to happen."

"Now." Molokai backed her up, steadying his gun.

"There's a bomb on a bus," Karin said. "Please help us."

It could have gone several different ways. If the gang rushed in, Hayden saw a blood bath ensuing. If they remained at stalemate, she'd have to cart some of them off to a police station. These scenarios only served to put people at risk. Remembering her CIA training and all the missions since she walked right up to Eastwood, lowering her gun.

"It's not for me or you. It's for innocent people. We'll take this explosives bastard down, I promise you. There won't be more than a few pieces left for the rats to chew on."

"You're gonna take the whole operation out?" Eastwood studied her. "That'd be interesting."

"No mercy," Hayden said. "No fooling around. We'll just . . . raze him."

Eastwood looked impressed. "Like the sound of that. Tonight?"

Hayden leaned up close. "Make those you trust help you. Keep everyone here and away from their phones for an hour. He must have no warning. Now—name and address."

Eastwood dropped his head so nobody could see his lips and whispered. "Crazy mother called Fuse, 'cause he loves the dynamite. Blew two fingers away years ago so you'll know him. No hair. Stick thin. Lives over in Whitney." He gave her an address.

"That's his house?"

"No, his yard."

"And he'll be there now?"

"Dude lives there. He's home, trust me."

Hayden turned and moved away. Molokai and Kinimaka covered her, but Eastwood was already deploying trusted men to police his own acolytes, shouting for phones and cooperation. Hayden reached the car and jumped in. Kinimaka climbed behind the wheel and started the engine.

"Where to?"

Hayden punched it into the satnav. "Drive."

They arrived twenty minutes later. Hayden spent the time trying to reach Paulson, but a second in command assured her there were no new developments. The buses hadn't been identified and were already nearing Los Angeles. She had to hurry.

Kinimaka pulled up at the curb. Ahead and to the left was a high solid fence and a slatted gate. A concrete drive ran down beyond that, all the way to a shabby looking warehouse at the bottom. All manner of goods littered the yard area around it, from the rusting hulks of cars to a crusher and old dumpsters. Hayden spied one CCTV camera mounted on a tower that covered the entire yard. Nobody was around although they could see a light shining inside the warehouse, its glow seeping through cracks in the warehouse's metal walls.

Without a word the team exited the car. Kinimaka ran on ahead, checking the padlock on the gate. Molokai reversed his weapon and smashed it off with the butt of his gun. The man's robes were higher tonight, perhaps to ward off the slight chill in the air, perhaps to guard against any light that may invade his vision.

Hayden wasn't sure, but she was glad he was along.

She approached with Karin and Dino as Kinimaka swung the gate open.

"Speed and surprise," she said. "Kill anyone you have to, but not Fuse."

They ran down the slope in silence. Hayden listened at the warehouse's door, hearing no sound. Within seconds, Molokai had reached a side door, stepped back and kicked it in. Without pause, he entered. Hayden raced to back him up.

Inside, it was a deadly turmoil.

She counted eight figures. Two were asleep on the floor. Four were rising to their knees. Two were rolling on the ground, reaching for weapons. Nobody looked scared or even shocked. These were hardened criminals.

Hayden let Molokai, Karin and Dino take point, as she searched for Fuse. For now, he had to live. The trouble was everyone was moving fast, and she needed to find cover. She positioned herself behind a low storage container, scanning for the man as fast as she could.

Shots rang out. Molokai, Karin and Dino had the element of surprise and precious seconds in which to aim. Their first three bullets struck flesh, killing two men and wounding another. Return fire hit machinery, bags of cement and brick support pillars. Hayden shot a fourth man through the head as she searched.

The last four were getting it together. Their firepower

was immense. Hayden saw two men with HK semi-autos in each hand firing hard at Molokai. It was then she spotted Fuse crawling toward a large metal box at the far end of the warehouse. Fittingly, he was as thin as a stick of dynamite with long hair and a bare chest. He wore shorts. Rubber bracelets covered his wrists in a sea of color. Hayden broke cover and ran down her side of the warehouse, keeping parallel with Fuse but on the other side.

Behind her, bullets riddled the machinery where Molokai had taken cover. Karin leaned out from behind a pillar, firing without pause, making the two men drop to the floor. Once they stopped firing Molokai was up and changing cover, finding a new spot and a new angle. Of the five men left including Fuse he then killed another. Karin shot the already wounded man on the floor.

Hayden slowed. Shots were still being fired but Fuse only had two cohorts left alive. She crossed the warehouse in Fuse's blind spot, reaching him just as he wrenched open the iron box.

Hayden saw dozens of black iron guns, the pile several feet high. On top of them, thrown in loosely, were layers of grenades and spare magazines. She was shocked at the amount of contraband inside, but held the barrel of her gun at Fuse's right temple.

"Don't move."

Fuse stiffened but didn't step back. Hayden saw his hands still brushing the top of the box. She rapped the gun barrel across the top of his head.

"Hands up."

He spun, striking with his palms, knocking the gun away. He grabbed her wrist and wrenched, pulling a muscle. His spare fist smashed into her face, making her see stars. She staggered, trying to pull the gun barrel away and regain control. Fuse was still close to the metal box and reached inside now, grabbing for a grenade.

"No!"

Hayden relinquished her hold on the gun. With two hands free she attacked. She targeted Fuse's wrist as he picked up the grenade, smashing it against the top of the box. Her other fist smashed into his throat. He reeled but still managed to scoop up one of the pineapple-shaped bombs.

Hayden spun into his body, back first, grabbed hold of the hand that held the grenade, dipped a shoulder and then threw him over. He landed heavily on his spine. The grenade rolled away, but Fuse was up in a second, reaching for it.

Tough bastard.

Hayden plucked out her Glock and shot him through the hand.

Fuse screamed as the ragged hole appeared in the meat of his right hand, but still tried reaching for the grenade with his left.

Hayden fired a bullet through that one too.

Fuse yanked his hands into his stomach, writhing and crying with pain. Hayden saw his two colleagues killed by Karin and Dino, and then Molokai raced toward her.

"You okay?"

She kicked Fuse in his right knee. "Yeah, this piece of shit would rather explode than talk."

Molokai turned to Karin and Dino. "Check the rest of the place."

Hayden knelt beside Fuse, wincing at the smell of sweat that enveloped him and the rancid stench of his breath.

"You sold an explosive device, a chemical set-up, to this man." She waved Steele's new picture under his nose. "A

One Percenter. We want everything you've got on him. We want to know what chemicals were involved, what trigger mechanism was used, and how to safely and quickly defuse it."

"You're kidding?" Fuse spat. "You got techs for that shit."

"But if we have the right information, we can do it faster. And we have to do it faster."

"You can go fuck yourself, lady." Fuse's face was so twisted in agony she wasn't sure if he was scared or indifferent.

"I'll handle this." Molokai stepped forward, pulled on the man's arm and stepped on the bicep. Then, he placed his spare foot over the top of Fuse's damaged hand.

"You sing right now, higher than Ariana Grande," Molokai growled. "Or this gets a hell of a lot worse."

Hayden did a double-take, not used to such black humor coming from Molokai. Maybe he was finally loosening up. She checked the warehouse once more, pleased to see Karin and Dino returning and shaking their heads.

"Check the outside," she said.

Fuse struck out at Molokai's huge thigh with his least injured hand, then screamed as it hit hard muscle, sending slivers of pain up to his brain.

Hayden crouched. "Not especially bright, are you?" she asked. "Just tell us what we want, and I'll get you medical attention. If not, you'll lose the use of that hand."

"I already lost it, bitch."

Molokai leaned his weight forward, crushing the injured hand against the concrete floor. Fuse blew hard between his clenched teeth, eyes screwed shut.

"Give him a minute," Hayden said, and Molokai stepped off.

Fuse opened eyes full of hatred. "Who set me up? Who snitched on me?"

"Eastwood," Hayden said.

"That fucking asshole. He's dead, a dead man walking."

"Now you." Molokai tapped his trapped hand with the front sole of his boot.

"Ahhh."

Hayden pulled Molokai away. "We don't want him fainting on us."

Fuse glared at them, then lifted his hands so he could examine the holes. "What a fucking mess."

"Medical attention for information," Hayden said. "You might even get to use them again."

Grimacing from pain, Fuse began to speak. "It was them One Percenters. I saw them, I checked 'em out. Put two and two together. Big guy and a Marine. Marine called the moose Steele, just once, when Steele pissed him off. Aggressive guy, the Marine. When they thought I wasn't listening Steele whispered something. He said: 'I guess we can take this to the Main Street depot now.' Marine told him to shut the hell up. They checked me out, but I pretended I hadn't heard."

Karin and Dino joined them. Karin carried her cellphone in her hand and checked it now. "Main Street depot," she said. "It's a bus station."

"The bus station," Dino said. "Surely that narrows the number of buses down? They didn't all start from that depot."

Hayden wasn't finished. "What else did these customers say?"

"Hey, they weren't running their mouths all night, bitch. They came and they went. Ten minutes."

Hayden bit her tongue. "And the explosives?"

"Yeah, yeah, I made them. They're in a metastable state, which means they'll only react to mechanical shock, friction or heat."

"React?" Dino asked.

"Explode. Obviously, I strapped a few pounds of C4 to them." Fuse couldn't hide a grin. "There's your heat."

"And the trigger mechanism?"

"Easy. A basic cellphone. A burner strapped to the C4. All you do to disable it is cut the wire. No trip wires. No tamper switches. They asked for a simple set up, they got a simple set up."

"Your bomb's now attached to a bus," Hayden told him. "When its engine turns off everyone explodes."

Fuse pursed his lips and nodded. "Sounds like a great plan."

Hayden drew her Glock and shot him through the face.

CHAPTER TWENTY FIVE

Drake pushed the car hard through the long, intense night. Man and machine, honed, raced the dawn, chasing the dreadful unknown with hope, determination and a little fear in his heart.

Fear for all the bus passengers.

An hour from Los Angeles, the news came in. Hayden and the others had narrowed the buses down to just three possibilities by finding out which depot the One Percenters had used.

Hayden updated them through their cells. "One bus is on the I10, passing Pomona. The second's on the I10, around Montclair. The third's slightly further back, passing the Euclid intersection. I have locations for all of you. Luther's way ahead. Dahl's next and then Drake's two minutes behind him. There's literally fourteen minutes between all three buses. And—" Hayden sighed "—they're all headed for the same depot."

Drake whistled. "Shit, which one."

"Downtown," Hayden said. "I'll send you the coordinates."

Drake calculated how far behind he was and put his foot down. "I'm chasing you down, Dahl," he said. "You'd better stop flirting and get your foot down."

"You stand about as much chance as a tramp on Wall Street. Come and get me."

Their engines roared. Drake thought he could see the Swede's taillights as they tore through the night. He switched the music to a rock channel, getting some adrenalin pumping. The first song that played was Deep

Purple's *Smoke on the Water*, which put him right up to Dahl's rear fender in under three minutes.

He slowed for traffic. They drove quickly but courteously. A faint dawn was cracking the darkness in half. The growling engine and the speed, coupled with the heavy, rhythmic music, gave him an intense focus the like of which he'd never felt in a car before. The jag felt alive, a part of him, receptive to his every thought. He pulled alongside Dahl and then eased back. Kenzie waved from the passenger seat; a rather surreal sight to be fair. Hayden informed them they were only four minutes behind Luther.

They blasted along the I10, Drake and Dahl riding together, one alongside the other, chasing the big G-Wagon as the dawn rose to the east.

Hayden called them once more. "The buses are approaching the depot. The police have it surrounded. We know the two One Percenters, the Fabergé eggs, and a bomb's on board. We think it's the silver bus, but aren't sure since none of the drivers have answered their phones. Do you see a silver bus?"

Drake did. Its high sides glinted as the first rays of sunlight flashed over the horizon. The black G-Wagon was tucked in behind it. The windows Drake could see were darkly tinted. He gunned the Jag alongside the suspect bus and looked up at the passengers. Some faces stared out, but mostly all he could see were vague shapes. He passed the bus and tucked in ahead.

"Want me to signal the driver?" He could see the man in his rearview.

"No," Hayden said. "They're gonna do that now as the buses pull into the depot."

"It's gonna be chaos, but you know our two super-thieves aren't gonna want to blow that bus up? This is part of their plan."

"Clearly. But after talking to the other three I believe they will if they have to. At least, the man called Jax will."

Drake gripped the wheel harder. The satnav told him he was four minutes from his destination. He saw a blue sports car out of the corner of his eye and then Dahl was traveling alongside him, to the left of the bus.

"You ready for this, pal?"

Dahl looked across. "I wish I had a baseball bat for that bomb."

It was a standing joke ever since the Swede had foiled a nuclear explosion in New York by hitting the device with a big hammer.

"You could always use Kenzie," Alicia said. "If you're looking for something thick, hard and pretty numb."

"Thought you were doubled over in the back seat," Kenzie hissed back.

"Only when Torsty asks nicely."

"Hey!" Drake said.

Mai jumped in. "She's definitely struggling back there. I think we've found something that keeps Taz quiet. For the most part."

"Then it's more road trips," Kenzie said, and nobody argued.

Then Drake took a deep breath. "Two minutes out, people. Game faces on."

CHAPTER TWENTY SIX

Drake pulled ahead of the silver bus, knowing there were two others ahead and they hadn't managed to identify the right one. He saw the big bus depot now: a central hub with the blue Greyhound logo across its fascia, and dozens of bus lanes, parking spots and bus stops. Many buses were already there, idling. Drake saw no sign of people, which was good, and no drivers sat waiting.

He came in hot, and was directed to a parking area where dozens of cop cars already sat askew, as if they'd been driven in hard and abandoned. There was a huge contingent of SWAT, FBI, cops and dozens of other unknown agencies gathered behind three closely parked, unmarked black vans. Drake stopped the car and jumped out, pocketing the keys just in case he needed them later. He looked back the way he'd come. The silver bus was driving down a ramp, preparing to enter the bus depot, its sides gleaming. Dahl was just pulling up.

Where the hell was Luther?

He switched his gaze to the left. The other two suspect buses had been directed into two parking bays and were coming to a stop. Luther's G-Wagon was about twenty feet from them.

Mai and Alicia were climbing out the doors.

It was crazy and fluid; the desperate scenario out of control. Drake saw the silver bus pulling in and being directed close to the other two. He could see drivers sitting behind their wheels, stretching, fiddling with their controls.

No!

Drake ran toward the danger, seeing Dahl, Alicia and

Mai doing the same. Already, cops were sprinting ahead of them, trying to attract the driver's attention without alerting the passengers. It was assumed that the One Percenters would be expecting a gun-toting reception committee and would be ready, but no policeman or agent in the world would let that stop them trying to save the passengers. Drake's breathing was strained with the tension, his legs aching from the long journey. His heart was in his mouth.

The silver bus pulled up. The driver stared at all the activity.

Drake waved at the man, mouthing the words "keep engine running." The driver shook his head, indicated that he couldn't hear, and reached forward as if to switch off.

"NO!" Drake screamed. "Leave the fucking key alone!"

The man sat back, scared, but still shaking his head. Drake saw passengers craning their necks. Cops and agents were surrounding the silver bus, ready to make a move. Everyone was horrifyingly aware that any one of the buses could explode at any time. Again, the silver bus's driver reached forward, eyes wide, a look of real terror on his face. Drake shook his head violently. He was desperate, but what could he do? Frantically, he fired into the air.

"No!"

Then a cop barged him aside, holding up a large piece of paper. On it were scribbled the words: *Leave engine running.*

"About . . . fucking . . . time," Drake panted.

Passengers stood and walked down the aisles of all three buses. The drivers sat tensely, looking scared. Their doors were still closed. Drake saw faces staring out of every window. Agents wearing bomb vests rolled underneath the buses, three at a time at front, middle and back. He saw high-powered rifles trained on the bus windows, their users seeking out just two heads among dozens.

"Get them off," he cried. "Get the passengers off now."

The cops were already on it. The drivers of all three buses responded to a coordinated signal and opened their doors. Passengers stepped off, instantly pulled away by waiting policemen. Every face was scanned as it appeared at the top of the steps and matched to the photos taken at the tech research lab.

Drake watched the driver of the silver bus closely. His lips were moving. The guy was trying to tell him something.

He stared, then squinted. *No mule? No school? Low fool?*

Then it hit him.

Low fuel.

Fuck!

He shouted it out, making sure every cop in the vicinity heard and then addressed the driver again. "How much?"

The man shrugged and held up ten fingers.

Their difficulties had multiplied. An agent shouted for a fuel truck. One of the bomb techs rolled out from underneath the silver bus, shaking his head.

The driver stiffened. Drake saw a man he recognized as Jax leaning forward, encircling the driver's throat with a big arm and waving a cellphone in the air. All activity stopped.

Drake looked left. Mai and the rest of the crew were helping passengers off the bus, dragging them in some cases. When Luther turned and caught his eye Drake made a covert signal.

Here.

Words were spoken and the entire Strike Force team started over.

Drake watched Jax mouth something. He didn't

understand it. Several cops shook their hands and held their hands up. Jax cursed, snarling. Drake saw the man as he really was: on the ragged edge. This situation could very easily and very quickly go either way.

Jax raised a gun and fired, blowing out the front windows of the bus. Glass exploded all over the gathered cops. Drake ducked as shards landed on the front of his jacket.

"Can you hear me now?" Jax shouted.

"Yes, yes," someone answered.

"I said get those bomb techs out from under the bus or I'll blow it. Do it!"

Drake saw one of the agents thumb his radio. Jax dragged the driver to the side window, watching as the bomb techs rolled out empty-handed. One, a blond-haired man, shook his head and gave them a look of despair.

"Now," Jax cried. "Step back. All of you. I want ten feet of clear space all the way around this bus."

Drake retreated as the gathered cops and agents started to form a wide cordon around the bus. Their best guess was that there were fifteen hostages on the bus, including the driver. They hadn't seen Cara yet, but assumed she was inside somewhere.

One of the cops shouted: "Low fuel."

Jax glanced at the dashboard in front of him and whispered to the driver. The man nodded, lips drawn tight.

"Then you'd better do as you're told," Jax shouted, "and quickly."

Drake saw the others walking up. Alicia nodded. The rest stood around him.

"That Jax?" Dahl's question was rhetorical. "What's he looking like mentally?"

Drake didn't sugar-coat it. "I think he'd blow that thing in a second."

"But it doesn't add up," Mai said. "If they're good enough to pull off eight of the greatest heists in history they can't be this highly strung. This volatile. I studied their previous robberies on the way here. They're dependable, cool and incomparable at what they do."

"I agree," Dallas said. "You can apportion a part of this to them never resorting to a Plan B before. To getting disrupted. But not all of it."

"You're saying they're not the One Percenters?" Dahl asked.

"No. I'm saying there's more to this than anyone knows. Maybe more than some of the One Percenters know."

Drake stepped forward. "We need to talk to Jax."

Alicia moved too, but Mai pulled her back.

"I don't think so, Taz."

"What?" Alicia's face was full of surprise. "You're saying I can't talk to a bell end with a bomb at the end of his stupid finger? Why?"

"You just explained it yourself."

CHAPTER TWENTY SEVEN

Drake moved forward but Jax moved away. The entire contingent of cops and agents peered harder, trying to track where the man went, but the bus's interior was dark and soon swallowed him up in shadow. As Drake watched, several passengers were manhandled to the front of the bus. He counted at least seven at the front, blocking all view of the aisle and the interior.

Drake turned. "What now?"

Minutes passed. The bus sat with its engine idling, running out of gas. Someone shouted it had about five minutes left. The gas truck was two minutes away. An agent walked up to the blasted front window and asked for permission to fuel the bus.

The passengers stared forward. Drake assumed they'd been ordered to do so. Another minute passed.

The driver shouted: "We're below the fucking red line. Way below."

The bus chugged, coughing on fumes. Had Jax decided to fade away, to let it blow? The thought sent spikes through Drake's heart and shivers down his spine.

The fuel truck arrived, slowing only as it approached the bus, tires squealing. Cops darted out of the way, one man diving and rolling to avoid its big wheels. It pulled up alongside the bus, leaving barely any gap. The driver jumped out and unreeled a thick hose with a pump attachment at the end.

The agent repeated his question.

Again, there was no answer. Drake stared at the passengers. Some were crying. A woman was hyperventilating. The driver was practically standing, ready to leap through the shattered window. Dahl went right up to the front, so close he could touch the metal.

Nobody wanted to make the call.

Drake saw it in the agents, in the cops, in the other FBI figures standing around. They knew what had to be done. But if they were wrong, their career and especially their conscience would never recover.

Drake nodded at Dahl and shouted: "Let's get these passengers off now. Get fuelling, and Bomb Guy: get under that bus!"

Everyone surged forward. Mai and Luther sprinted for the door just as the driver opened it. The driver himself leapt through the front window, grazing himself and breaking his arm when he landed, but was otherwise okay. The bus chugged and rattled, gulping down its last fumes of diesel.

Passengers exited and ran for their lives in every direction. Mai and Luther helped them while Alicia, Kenzie and Dallas watched out for Jax and Cara. People were crying, screaming. Drake helped two men down from the front of the bus. Dahl sprinted to the spot where the blond-haired bomb tech had rolled under and threw himself to the ground.

"Where are we?"

"Almost there. I practically had it last time."

"How long?"

"Half a minute."

Fuck, Drake thought. *It's gonna be close.*

The bus rattled. Nobody had seen Jax or Cara yet. Was this part of their plan, this close call with the fuel? The man with the diesel hose had unfurled it all the way around the truck and was wrenching the bus's filler cap open. Mai and

Luther continued to drag passengers clear. FBI agents and cops helped them. Others had gone to search the other two buses as an afterthought.

Nine passengers were clear. Drake saw the last three people gathering at the top of the exit steps. He drew his Glock and moved up close to the damaged front window.

Nothing moved along the dark aisle or at the back of the bus. Jax and Cara had to be hiding in one of the seats.

But why?

He checked the perimeter. It looked good. Men encircled the bus right up to the fuel truck. Mai and Luther helped the last three passengers off and glanced at Drake. Luther spread his hands.

Dahl leapt to his feet. "Bomb defused!"

The bus sipped on its last vestiges of fuel, but now fresh diesel was being sprayed into the tank. Drake felt a huge rush of relief and then adrenalin.

"Storm those bastards," somebody said.

FBI agents raced past Mai and Luther, guns drawn, proceeding carefully up the steps, onto the bus. Drake found an area along the bottom of the windshield that was clear of broken glass and hauled himself up. Dahl was a second behind him. Together, they stood in the space around the driver's seat.

Two agents stalked the aisle ahead of them.

"Stand up," one shouted. "Raise your hands. It's over."

They walked further down the aisle. Drake and Dahl joined the procession, checking every seat and the spaces underneath.

Nothing.

They walked slowly and cautiously all the way to the back of the bus. They checked the toilet. And then they turned and stared at each other, nonplussed. For a moment nobody spoke.

An agent raised a radio to his mouth. "Bus is empty," he said, with utter disbelief.

Drake stared at Dahl. "I don't get it."

A voice squawked a reply over the radio. "Say again? What did you say?"

"I said the bus is empty," the agent repeated. "They're gone."

Drake collapsed into a seat. The Fabergé eggs were gone too.

But how?

CHAPTER TWENTY EIGHT

A silence as cold as a polar vortex descended over the bus.

Everyone stared at each other rather than looking for an explanation as to what had happened. It was Dahl and Luther that moved first. One turned to the lead FBI agent and one spoke up.

"Get searching," Luther said. "They may have come from Vegas, but I never noticed Siegfried or Roy with them." When some men looked blank Luther explained: "They were masters of illusion."

"Bomb squad," Dahl said. "For all we know there's more than one bomb."

A veil of fear fell across several faces. It was dark and air conditioned on the bus. The engine was still running and sounding much healthier now that it had a new supply of life juice.

Drake highly doubted there'd be more than one bomb. He trusted Hayden and the others to have checked for that information. It was mostly Dahl's way of motivating people, he knew. Probably not the best way, but then it was Dahl.

Men were on their knees and crawling under seats. Drake moved to the rear of the bus where they'd last seen Jax. Alicia was at his back and Mai at hers. Kenzie and Dallas were close to the driver's seat.

A cop, crawling out from a foot well, noticed it. "Hey," he said.

Drake heard and looked over but nobody else did.

"Hey." The rough edge of panic made his throat sound raw.

Now more men looked over. Drake and Dahl strode toward him.

Dahl saw it first. "Oh, no."

Drake dropped to his knees, examining the floor. "This is great," he said. "Why didn't anyone else think of this?"

He remembered Jax pushing all the passengers to the front of the bus. He remembered Jax melting back into the shadows. He now knew why nobody had spotted Jax and Cara escaping.

There was a large, rectangular trapdoor in the floor of the bus.

"It's for maintenance," a cop said helpfully.

Dahl wrenched on the hatch, pulling it open. He held on to the sides and looked underneath. After a second, he lowered himself to the ground. Drake followed, hit by a blast of warm air. He shuffled forward as Alicia and Mai joined them.

Dahl was performing a full three-sixty. "Daylight to all sides," he said. "Except there."

He pointed. The right side of the bus appeared to be longer than all the others. He could see daylight, but it was much further away.

"What the hell?"

Dahl started to crawl in that direction. Drake and the others followed, constantly joined by more cops and agents. Several minutes later they were nearing daylight and pulling themselves to their feet.

Drake squinted a little at first as the bright sunlight hit his eyes. The first thing he thought was: *Where is everybody?*

He turned and saw the vehicle behind him. It was the fuel truck. The dread certainty of what had happened struck his brain.

"They crawled under the bus and then under the fuel truck. The cops had surrounded the bus not the fuel truck."

"Jax let the bus run low on purpose," Dahl said. "He wanted the fuel truck."

"Bold plan," Mai whistled. "They took a chance."

"That's pretty much all they've done on this job," Alicia said. "After such a perfect robbery."

Drake surveyed the bus station's open lot. "Yeah, something's up with them. They're ticking fucking time bombs. So, where'd they go?"

Dahl was dragging the lead FBI man onto his feet.

"Hey, steady, man," the agent spluttered.

Dahl pointed into the air. "Those are your choppers, right?"

"Yeah."

"They didn't notice two people crawling out from here and walking away?"

The agent's mouth tightened. "I suspect, like all of us, they were at the other side of the bus helping the passengers get clear and waiting for the bomb to explode. They'd have pulled back."

Dahl saw the logic in it. "They have CCTV?"

"Yeah."

"Get on it right now. We need to know where Jax and Cara went."

The agent didn't waste any time barking out orders. Drake noticed several new choppers arriving, probably news outlets. There would definitely be some tense stories to be told today.

"They're running the footage through up there," the agent told them, "in-situ. Get ready."

Drake guessed Jax and Cara had an eight- to ten-minute head start.

More and more police were joining them on this side of the fuel truck. Choppers beat at the skies above. Traffic streamed by on a nearby highway. Buses continued to come and go at the front of the station. Drake saw dozens of civilians pointing cameras in their direction. It was a tense, powerless few minutes. Like many others, he used them to check his weapons and other gear. He even managed to find out the lead FBI agent's name: Cooper.

Alicia nudged him. "Still haven't used my weapon," she said.

"Don't worry. I get the feeling there's more to this than we're seeing."

Cooper showed them a tablet computer. "Here's the footage."

They crowded round. Drake saw two figures at the far end of the screen, emerging from underneath the fuel truck. They walked to the far end of the bus station where they climbed into a car. The car then drove away, joining a road that led right past the depot.

"Can you zoom in?" Luther asked.

"Yeah, we got the registration. It's a Chevy Equinox, dark red. The upside to all this is . . . they think they got away."

"They did," Dahl said. "Now we have to track them down."

"There are thousands of cameras across this city," Cooper said. "Hundreds of thousands. We'll find them."

As if to confirm his words, the tablet flashed onto a new screen. Someone was feeding it remotely. They saw a photographic still. It was grainy, but it showed a car with the right registration cruising through a set of traffic signals.

"Venice Boulevard," Cooper said. "It's five minutes from here by air. Ten by car."

Dahl looked up into the air. "Get those birds down fast."

Cooper shouted more orders. Three choppers swooped

down, their rotors churning the air as they bounced softly upon the depot's parking lot. Noise surrounded them. The Strike Force team split and ran toward all three choppers, followed by the most senior FBI agents and SWAT. Cooper was radioing for more SWAT teams to meet them en route. Drake jumped into a helicopter amid the chaos and strapped in. This time Mai was at his side. Alicia ended up somewhere else, he couldn't see.

"You coping?" Mai asked seriously above the noise as other's jumped inside.

Drake sighed. "Yeah, she's hard to keep up to and impossible to reason with but she has a big heart."

Mai looked blank. "What?"

"Alicia."

"No," the Japanese woman grinned, "although I'm looking forward to telling her all that. You make her sound like a racehorse."

"Shit," Drake turned wide eyes on her. "Please don't tell her I said that."

Mai gave him a look he remembered well. It meant: Maybe I will, maybe I won't. It wasn't a good sign. "What the hell did you mean?" he asked.

"The new life followed by this. It's had an impact on all of us."

"Did you settle in okay?"

"I had Luther. And Chika, and Dai, and Grace. Time flew."

Drake nodded.

"You only had Alicia."

He looked up. "I'm not rising to that bait." He held on tight as the chopper rose. "I missed this," he said. "Missed the team. The banter. The company. I'm not sure I'm cut out for vacation time."

"Vacations are harder than I thought," Kenzie said from the seat opposite. "But I am enjoying being part of the new task force."

"Yeah." Drake nodded at her. "I never would've predicted that."

"My family's headed to Stockholm soon," Dahl said from the fourth seat. "So I guess I know where I'll be vacationing next time."

Drake held Dahl's eyes but didn't say anything. There were few words that could help any man or woman at that point of their lives. Dahl knew they were there if he needed them.

The helicopter flew over Rosa Parks Freeway toward Culver City. The vast city spread out in all directions with the ocean to their left. The chopper dipped as it crossed Jefferson and then Culver. Three more birds flew along with them. The pilots were shouting into their radios and checking their navigation.

Soon they were swooping over Venice Boulevard.

"How we doing?" Drake leaned forward, asking Cooper in one of the front seats.

"I can see them."

CHAPTER TWENTY NINE

Four choppers swooped through the skies, noses down. On board, SWAT, FBI agents and the Strike Force prepped weapons and gear. Everyone could see Venice Boulevard now, four lanes wide at this point, bordered by strip malls, office blocks and houses as it arrowed west toward the ocean. Gas stations and car dealerships boasted bright, multi-colored signs, along with fast-food restaurants. Drake saw traffic signals hung on long metal arms that crossed the street, making helicopter flying hazardous. Still eyeing the Chevy Equinox, he saw cop cars and motorcycles streaming in from side streets, red and blue lights flashing. This was about to get very dangerous and very loud.

The occupants of the Equinox caught on. The vehicle put on a burst of speed and weaved through traffic. Drake's helicopter swooped as low as the pilot dared, almost skimming the top of the traffic signals. By now, they were over the Equinox.

"Six black-and-whites," Mai said. "Four bikes, and four helicopters. I doubt even the One Percenters planned for that."

"They're not stopping," Kenzie said.

Drake tapped his comms button to make sure it was working. The police cars below were practically tailgating the Equinox as it swept through traffic. Ahead a signal was at red. Drake cringed as the Equinox raced straight through, causing a collision between three other cars that had to swerve. The police were forced to slow, the motorbikes weaving their way through moving cars.

"It's bedlam," Alicia said on the comms. "Get me down there."

Drake knew that wasn't an option. They'd lose all touch with the chase by the time they landed and found another vehicle. They were airborne until the Equinox stopped.

Cooper glared down through an open window at the front. "That's just fucking crazy."

The Equinox slewed to avoid a car that flew out of a side-street without checking, clipped another car's rear end, and veered into the opposite lane. For long seconds it dodged oncoming vehicles, swinging left and right, before crossing the middle of the road once more and resuming its sprint. Its pursuers lost more ground, but the choppers kept up, especially Drake's which slid around an eight-foot-high sign with a golf ball on top, almost sideways, like a car would drift around a corner.

Drake let out a whistle of appreciation. "That was good."

"Drake," Alicia came onto the comms. "I've said it before, and I'll say it again. Your chopper's awesome."

Drake managed to keep the smile off his face. Mai didn't acknowledge the words.

Cooper's cell rang. He held it to his ear and listened for a few minutes. Drake saw his shoulders droop as he shook his head.

"That's not possible," he said twice in a row. "That's just not possible."

Drake's wariness soared. Mai glanced at him, worry in her eyes. Another minute passed before Cooper ended the call.

"What is it?" Dahl asked.

"You won't believe it," Cooper appeared to be in shock. "It doesn't make any sense."

"What?" Drake asked.

"They got away."

Drake stared at him in astonishment, then turned his

eyes to the Equinox below. "You mean they're not driving?"

Cooper shook his head. "I don't mean Jax and Cara. I mean the other three."

Drake struggled to get his head around it. "The other . . . wait, you mean in Las Vegas?"

"Kushner, Faye and Steele. They escaped."

"It's not possible."

"This Faye, she's a computer genius. Apparently, they knew which police station they'd be taken to in advance—the closest one to Caesars. She'd built a redundancy into the station's system for a certain time. When that time came around all the systems shut down. Cell doors opened. *Every* door opened. Building went black. The One Percenters were ready for it and made their escape."

"That's why they were researching that station." Drake remembered their first few clues.

"Yeah, some street fighting gang got them the station's info. They had men on the inside, prisoners, that gave them the layout. Faye just spliced into the mainframe and shut it down. They escaped along with a dozen others."

"Any clues as to where they're headed?" Kenzie asked.

Cooper looked at the Equinox below. "Best guess? To meet up with these two dickheads."

"When did it happen?" Mai asked.

"Over an hour ago," Cooper said. "The cops in Vegas have been chasing their tails, sorting shit out at their own end trying to capture dangerous convicts. Three thieves didn't register so high until they heard about all this."

"So if they'd prearranged a private plane?" Drake voiced the most obvious scenario.

Copper checked his watch. "They'll be landing any minute."

Drake called Hayden. "You heard, love?"

"Yeah we just heard the news. We'll be with you soon."

"You will?"

"There was no point hanging around Vegas, so we jumped on a plane."

"Cool, we'll be somewhere between Santa Monica and Hawaii."

Hayden laughed. "Is it that bad?"

"Oh, it's much worse."

Drake described the situation as their helicopters flew above the speeding vehicle. A barrage of cop cars flew after it, spread out over ten city blocks. Their gaudy red and blue lights painted buildings and signs and windows for miles around. Motorcycles nipped in between them, two even now motoring right up to the Equinox.

The speeding car veered sharply. One rider was struck, his bike falling and sliding with him still on board, hitting a curb and then vaulting up and across a garden, leaving a wide, ragged trail of mud in its wake. The second bike swerved and had to jam on its brakes to avoid a head on collision. Two cop cars pulled out of the chase to help.

"Why aren't they blocking the road?" Hayden asked.

"They did. Jax just drove onto the other side of the road and almost killed two people. It's too dangerous and he's going too fast."

"He has to run out of road soon."

"Yep, or he's got a submarine waiting."

Hayden promised to seek them out as soon as they landed. Drake wondered what more could go wrong. Had they lost all the One Percenters and the eggs?

Where was Jax going?

One of the choppers tried to swing around in front of Jax's car, its skids practically touching the windshield. They were trying to put Jax off, a risky move at this speed.

Ahead, a junction came up fast, this one blessedly without a stop light. Drake's chopper swooped down to the left of the car as another slammed against its roof, four motorcycles blasting along just behind its rear fender.

They blasted through the junction at speed. Traffic had been stopped and Drake saw people getting out of their cars, openmouthed at the spectacle of speed-racing through their city.

Drake's pilot backed off. The Equinox plowed down Venice toward the ocean, now only minutes from the beach.

"It's one way ahead," the pilot said.

"You think they care about that?" Cooper said. "Stay on them."

From their aerial view, Drake saw a wide, paved walkway ahead fronting a vast expanse of warm yellow sand and then the sparkling blue ocean. Jax was headed right toward it.

"It's very odd," Dahl said.

"They're communicating with someone," Cooper told them. "Phone's been hot for fifteen minutes."

"I can't imagine what they could do next," Mai said.

Drake glared at her. "C'mon, Mai. Don't bloody jinx it."

As if in answer, their world went crazy.

CHAPTER THIRTY

The sparkling ocean burst into full view ahead, spanning their vision to left and right. A flat expanse of gray paving and then sandy beach led right to it, dotted by palm trees, bike stands and a refreshments shack.

"We have speedboats waiting on the water," Cooper said.

There was nowhere for Jax to go. Their plan was unfathomable. Were they just desperate, driving as far as they could until their colleagues caught up? They'd learned there was a private landing strip just a twenty-minute drive from here, and helicopter pads even closer, so expected the imminent arrival of the other three One Percenters.

What they didn't expect was what happened next.

Skimming the palm trees to their right came five more helicopters, flying side-by-side, spanning the width of the beach.

Cooper voiced his surprise and turned to the back. "Anything to do with you?"

Drake was stunned and looked it.

"They must be here for Jax," Mai said.

"No way," Cooper said. "No fucking way."

It all twisted out of kilter again. The Equinox veered onto the paved walkway, heading straight for the oncoming choppers. From out of the chopper doors appeared a deadly array of guns.

"What the . . ." Dahl muttered.

There were no warning shouts. The new arrivals opened fire. Drake cringed. Bullets crashed around the fleeing car, into the concrete paving, and among the stores to the right. Jax somehow kept to a straight line.

"Look out!" Kenzie cried.

The attacking birds flew straight at their own, peeling away seconds before impact. The occupants continued shooting, firing at both the Equinox and Drake's helo. Bullets ricocheted off the metal frame. Alicia's helicopter went high and Dallas's went low. For one long minute there was total mayhem.

"There're choppers everywhere!" Alicia cried.

"Normally," Mai said, sighting her weapon. "You'd be up for that."

The new birds swung around in pursuit of Jax, swooping toward the ground, their noses angled. They skimmed the concrete walkway just yards above its surface. Everywhere, civilians ducked and dived away, falling amongst scattered chairs, tables and clothes racks, or ran for the beach. Drake's helo followed about thirty feet higher up.

"Anyone have the slightest clue what's going on?" Cooper asked.

"Not the foggiest, mate," Drake said, "but I think you're gonna need more men."

Cooper plucked out his phone. Mai fired on the new choppers from one side and Dahl did the same at the other. The stream of police and motorbikes was coming up behind them now, down to three cars and four bikes.

Ahead, bullets strafed the Equinox, punching holes through the back screen and the roof. The vehicle wobbled, spinning a full three-sixty before racing off again, its tires squealing, leaving rubber on the concrete. Mai hit one of the choppers, but her attack seemed to have no effect.

Two then swept down hard, striking the ground in front of the car with their skids before bouncing back up. Shots were punched into the car's windshield. The driver stamped on the brakes and sent it into a spin. The front end smashed through a shop window, still traveling straight, bringing the entire building down.

Then it stopped, shuddering, shot through with holes.

The doors flew open. All but one of the attacking choppers landed. That one stayed in the air and swung around toward the police choppers.

Cooper urged their helicopter to the ground. Drake leaned forward, trying to get a clearer view of what was happening. Two people jumped out of the red Equinox, a large, broad-shouldered man with stubble for hair, and a slim, blond-haired girl. That had to be Jax and Cara. Both wore backpacks. They carried weapons but threw them onto the floor. Cara was shouting something at Jax.

Drake peered harder.

The woman was flinging her arms around; her body language radiating anger. Jax was shouting back at her. The enemy choppers landed and disgorged their cargo. Drake counted a dozen men jumping out and running for the Equinox.

Their own skids hit the ground and settled. To left and right others did the same, and people prepared to exit. The collection of cop cars and bikes was screeching to a halt several yards behind.

Drake flicked his comms. "I don't know who we're supposed to be attacking here?"

Luther came back: "The eggs. Get the eggs. Destroy anything that gets in the way."

Typical Luther: destroy! But Drake agreed. He hefted his gun and jumped onto the concrete. At that moment a new voice entered his head.

"It's us," Hayden said. "We're landing behind you right now."

Booyah, Drake thought. *The team's all here.*

They paused by the choppers for twenty seconds. Jax and Cara were still fighting; their new, machine-gun toting enemies running in closer. Drake saw Cara step away from Jax and give a despairing glance back at the police. To Drake's mind she wanted to join them.

"Come on!" he shouted. "We've got you."

"Typical." Alicia was at his side. "Leave you alone for ten minutes and you're waving at a blonde."

He ignored her. Cara was turning their way, but then came the sound of a deep and deadly rising thunder. A buffeting cacophony as four more enemy helos roared in from the ocean. Two cut speed as they approached the police and one swooped down toward Jax and Cara.

They flew right in front of Drake. On board, in the back, he saw Kushner's face pressed against the window. He could just make out Faye too, her arms tied above her head. Both her and Kushner's faces were bloodied and beaten.

Guns were pointed at them.

The helicopter hovered a few feet off the ground, giving Jax and Cara the chance to see their captured colleagues.

"I have to say," Dahl said through the comms. "The only reasoning behind this new attack must be the Fabergé eggs."

He ducked as men from the new arrivals opened fire. Bullets peppered the choppers and police cars. Drake didn't take his eyes off the scene unfolding around Jax and Cara. The bird holding their colleagues lifted off. Attackers were now beside them, pulling their arms behind their backs and securing them. Guns were aimed at their heads. Spare men covered their comrades by laying down fire. The cops, firing back, took three down. To the left, toward the ocean, more gunfire was exchanged.

"We're up against a major criminal player here," Cooper

said. "To mount this kind of all-out surprise attack."

"Arms dealer? Gun runners?" Dahl asked.

"Maybe."

The war on Venice Beach continued under a bright, hot sun. Hayden and the others ran up and crouched down.

"Thought you'd be here," Kinimaka said.

"In the middle of the action?" Alicia asked.

"On the beach."

Drake rose and fired, running from cover to cover. He reached the Equinox with Dahl just as the gunmen grabbed their own helicopter to haul themselves inside. Jax and Cara were among them, being coerced none too gently with the butts of guns and fists. Drake rose and shot one enemy through the spine; Dahl picked off another. Return fire speckled the car. Drake ran to the front, peered out and killed another opponent.

Over ten enemy gunmen were dead now. The four extra choppers hovering to the ocean-side seemed to sense a shift in power and glided in closer, continuing their stream of fire. The force of their bullets knocked bikes over and perforated cars. Mai was concentrating on the lead bird, firing several shots before managing to hit the driver. It crunched nose-first into the beach, sending up a wave of sand, then exploded. Fire licked up from the wreckage, the flames reflected on the low undercarriages of its companions.

Drake kept firing but couldn't stop Jax and Cara being thrown into the helicopter. Men jumped after them. Dahl winged one, Drake killed another. The bird lifted off almost instantly, followed by the other three.

The birds near the ocean swung away too, just three now, still firing. Drake looked up and noticed for the first time that every chopper was worn, probably used every day and rarely serviced. A shout went up among those gathered around.

"After them."

It was every man for himself, everyone just trying to jump into a police chopper as they rose off the ground.

Drake found a place. So did Alicia, Kinimaka and Mai. Dahl couldn't get on board and ran for the closest police cruiser, radio in hand. He'd follow through the streets. Dallas, Karin and Dino were with him.

"Punch it, punch it!" Cooper cried. "We gotta catch those assholes."

CHAPTER THIRTY ONE

They swept along the coastline as it swung southeast, seven enemy helicopters and four flown by police. Cars tried to keep up with them along the highways but lost ground, as did motorbikes. Speedboats kept pace at sea, flying over the waves in pursuit of the action.

Men had secured themselves to bulkhead straps in the enemy choppers ahead and now leaned out, firing at their pursuers. Drake's helo swerved from side to side, eluding the bullets. It was only when a man leaned out with an RPG that Drake saw the gravity of what was happening.

"This is war. Whoever they are, they came prepared for anything. Drop back."

The rocket exploded from its housing, passing between the police helicopters and slamming down into the ocean. Alicia's bird pulled ahead, coming alongside their enemy, its occupants firing hard. The enemy pilot was hit and killed. The craft went out of control, spiraling down into the dazzling ocean, the waves swallowing it up.

Hayden was in the third chopper, urging her pilot to speed up. They were already screaming through the air, the noise tremendous. Speedboats raced below them. The highway was a sea of glittering police cars, still trailing. Hayden leaned out and lined up a shot, but a man trained his gun on her and fired, forcing her back inside. Drake heard her curse over the comms.

The chase continued to follow the coastline, passing over Redondo Beach and Long Beach without slackening its pace or changing course. It was only when they approached San Diego and Tijuana that the enemy helicopters veered to the left and headed inland.

"What are your orders?" Cooper was shouting into a radio.

Drake realized the man's authority had been exceeded by someone working remotely, from an office. On the ground.

It didn't surprise him.

They headed out across the southern Californian desert, over small mountain ranges, state parks and Native American reservations, leaving all other vehicles behind. They entered a mountain wilderness south of Borrego Springs. It was here, finally, that the choppers descended.

Drake tried to get a better view.

"We've got 'em," Cooper said a bit prematurely. "They're landing."

Nine helicopters swooped down toward the rolling sands and ragged peaks. Barren, gray vistas lay everywhere, a stark contrast to the cities of Los Angeles and Vegas. The lead six birds approached a flat landing area.

To Drake it looked pre-made, the whole thing pre-planned.

"I don't like the look—"

Camouflage netting was thrown back, revealing heavy-duty weapons. Dozens of armed men raced out of a nearby dry ravine bed.

Drake saw exactly what they were headed into.

"People," he said, "you'd better brace for hell."

CHAPTER THIRTY TWO

Three police choppers nose-dived at dozens of heavily armed men.

Bullets slammed into the cockpit and undercarriage. Drake flinched as a hole punched through the bulkhead next to his skull. Kenzie, seated beside him, fired back down, the sound of her semi-auto deafening inside the enclosed space. Their chopper veered to the left as Hayden's veered to the right.

But Alicia's kept on going, headed straight down at the shooters.

Alicia! Drake thought.

Luther and Mai were also on that helicopter. He wondered if Luther was calling the shots. Their own metal shell was spattered again, bullets glancing off. The ground rushed up fast. They were just twenty feet high now.

Alicia's bird bounced down into the sand at the center of the firing men. Two were struck by the skids and went down like rag dolls falling off a shelf. The chopper bounced back up and came down for a second time on top of a group of men. Bullets riddled its sides. Drake could see a trail of destruction in its wake: men, weapons and scorched earth.

As his own chopper touched down, bullets had stopped striking it. The enemy were concentrating on Alicia's chopper and in dragging the One Percenters away. He saw Jax and Cara thrown to the ground and then kicked. He saw Kushner punched and hauled across the rock-strewn desert by a huge man. He saw Faye and Steele pulled out of choppers at gunpoint. Faye complied but Steele struggled, and was tased for his troubles.

Their third chopper, with Hayden and Molokai on board, hit the desert floor away to the right. Drake was already in motion, jumping to the sandy ground on their bird's blind side, with Kenzie and three of the SWAT officers in tow.

He dropped to the floor. Dust plumed up all around them. Crawling forward, he finally understood what they had come upon.

No, we were led to this.

It looked like a sizeable force had been waiting in the desert. Upward of thirty men. They touted all kinds of weapons from handguns to RPGs. They weren't especially well protected—most wore T-shirts and shorts to be fair—but what they lacked in body armor they made up for in firepower. Drake spied five flat-bed trucks and four jeeps, all dusty and battered, lined up to one side.

They were facing south.

Drake knew what lay in that direction: Mexico. And it strengthened his suspicions of who these men might me. The One Percenters were being forcibly herded toward the vehicles. Alicia's chopper had finally grounded. Figures were jumping out of it and diving to cover. Hayden was pinned down to the far right of the area, using stones and hillocks for cover.

Drake saw no way to approach the enemy. No way to save the eggs or the thieves short of a risky all-out charge with guns blazing. Something he'd done before but not to save some works of art.

Wiping his face, he glanced around. Dust stuck to the sweat that coated his forehead. His boots scraped in the gravel as he moved. Behind them was a narrow, dry ravine, about the depth of a man. Drake swung his body into it, boots first, landing with a thud. Kenzie was at his back. Together they ran a hundred yards until they were behind a small mound of dirt. Drake stopped and carefully raised his head.

They were well behind the battle now. A slight slope led all the way to the top of a rock mound, about twenty feet in height. Drake saw only one problem: A guard crouched at the top of the rock mound, probably covering the rear.

Drake looked at Kenzie. "Let's go."

"On it."

Together they crawled over the smooth, dusty rock pile, staying low and quiet. Back here, the noise of the fight was muffled, even gunshots were muted. The man ahead had planted his gun beside him and was peering over the edge of the rock, watching the action rather than his peripheries.

Drake didn't want to shoot him in the back, so called out and took aim. "Hands up."

The man whirled and reached for his gun. Kenzie shot him through the forehead. Drake rose to his knees and ran the rest of the way in a crouch.

They peered over the rocky edge, right down on top of the battle.

It wasn't going their way. The One Percenters were at the pick-up trucks. Jax was already aboard. Kushner was being thrown in as they watched, his body doubled-over with pain. A man had Faye and was taunting her with his gun even as bullets whizzed around them. Somebody had killed two of the RPG-toting enemies, but they still had dozens of machine guns handy. Drake saw Steele standing his ground among the enemy and despite the weaponry, striking out with clenched fists, knocking men left and right. Someone fired a round into the ground between his legs, but Steele only bellowed and ran toward the shooter.

Drake grimaced. "That's one stupid man."

Kenzie tapped his shoulder. "Look."

He followed her finger. Cara had broken free and was running for Alicia's crashed helicopter. Drake could see Alicia and Luther making their way around to the front of the chopper, despite taking heavy fire.

Drake saw a chance. They could drop twenty feet onto the shooters standing between Cara and Alicia.

Nodding at Kenzie, he spoke quickly: "It's doable. We need Cara to know who these guys are and what they're planning for the eggs. And the One Percenters."

"Got it."

Drake secured his semi-auto over his shoulder and jumped first, landing atop one man and dragging two others down with him. Cara skidded to a stop just feet away, looking shocked. Kenzie landed next, taking two more men to the ground. Those still standing scrambled away. Two took bullets from Alicia and one from Luther. Drake struggled on the ground, covered in yellowish dust, scrabbling over the stones and gravel. His handgun was jammed into a man's stomach. He discharged it and pulled away, then rolled at a second man who was trying to gain his feet.

He went down and Drake grabbed his shirt, hauling himself atop the man. Kenzie punched her opponent, at the same time reaching for her gun that had fallen away. Men were rising all around and those that she and Drake hadn't felled were trying to get a bead on them. Cara was waiting, her hands clenched into fists, not sure where to run next.

Drake punched his man in the throat and face, then left him groaning. It was imperative to reach Cara before someone shot her. Alicia, Luther and three agents were starting to lay down good cover fire, making their enemy duck low or take cover. He reached Cara just as men peeled away from the fight at Hayden's chopper to chase the escaped One Percenter.

Drake rose to his feet just as they fired.

No!

He yanked Cara around, shielding her with his body. Two bullets struck him, their impacts like sledgehammers smashing into his body. Grateful for the body armor, Drake sprawled on the floor, gasping heavily.

Cara was lying right beside him, her face close to his. Blood coated her features. "Help us, it's the Ruiz cartel. They have Jax's wife."

Drake stared, unable to move. All this was for one man's wife? Another man's obscene wealth? Gathering strength, he forced his body off the ground.

A boot slammed him back down. An arm reached for Cara, dragged her up and then a gun was pointed at Drake's head. He could see the barrel close to his left eye.

"Die motherfu—"

The gun and the man lurched away as bullets slammed into him. More men fell to their knees around Cara, dragging her away, giving them no time for anything else.

Drake rolled over.

Carefully, he sat upright. To left and right the cartel men were down or running. They had everything they needed, it seemed. Kenzie was on all fours in the dirt, recovering from a blow across the head. Men lay groaning and bleeding everywhere. Alicia, Luther and SWAT guys were suddenly around them, and from the east came the men from Drake's chopper. Hayden and Mai were still trapped behind their bird.

The cartel men jumped behind the wheels of three flatbeds and two jeeps, most hiding in the back, forcing the One Percenters down and firing over the upraised sides. Drake crawled behind a dead man, using his body as cover. Everyone knelt and returned fire.

Drake suddenly saw Steele rise in the back of the last flat-bed. Somehow, they had managed to drag him over there, but he wasn't about to go down quietly. He was a hot-headed ex-Marine, Drake knew, that couldn't control his aggression. The kind of man that got others killed.

Steele lashed out left and right. A gun flew over the side of the flat-bed pickup. The vehicle slewed as it accelerated, making Steele fall to one knee. He struck another man on the temple, smashing him against the side of the truck. He kicked out, sending another into the back of the front cabin, breaking the rear window.

A shout went up. Drake couldn't make it out but guessed what it was a moment later. Bullets riddled Steele's chest. Blood poured down the front of his T-shirt as he pinwheeled his arms and staggered back, finally falling off the back of the truck. His lifeless body crashed to the ground.

Drake rose and walked across to Hayden. "We have a big problem," he said.

"You think?"

"No. It's worse. That's the Ruiz cartel. They're taking the eggs and the thieves to Mexico."

Hayden closed her eyes. "Shit."

Cooper, the lead FBI agent, was close by. "That puts it way out of our jurisdiction. We're done here."

He turned and walked away.

Drake could only stare at the plumes of dust marking the route of the getaway vehicles.

CHAPTER THIRTY THREE

Drake waited underneath the burning sun. He wiped sweat from his forehead and face. The plumes of dust were now barely discernible on the horizon.

Alicia came up to him. "Saw you get shot."

"Did you fire those bullets that saved me?"

"Nah, don't be daft. I knew you had it."

Drake made a face and looked to Luther. "You?"

"No. Must have been one of the SWAT guys."

Drake promised himself he'd thank them all. Hayden was already on her cellphone, trying to contact somebody that could make a critical decision. Drake shrugged his jacket off and stood there in his T-shirt, breathing heavily.

"Hey, watch out," Alicia said. "Easy to catch sunburn out here, Drakey."

"Oh, so you thought I could handle a bullet, but you warn me about the sun." Drake shook his head, turning away. He saw vehicles approaching from the east, but straight away could see Dahl in the lead car. The Swede was quickly out and running toward them with Dallas, Karin and Dino at his back.

"Everyone okay? What happened?"

"We're all good, "Drake responded. "Where the hell have you been? Didn't fancy the battle?"

"Oh, I fancied it all right. Especially when I heard you got shot."

Drake growled. "It wasn't much fun, mate, believe me."

"Not for you, maybe. I'd have enjoyed it though."

Drake couldn't stop the grin, but turned away, not giving Dahl the satisfaction of winning. Alicia filled Dahl in.

"Looks like the cartel boss kidnapped Jax's wife, forcing him to steal the eggs. Or he hijacked a plan that was already in place. Either way, it explains Jax's behavior and the One Percenters' unusual actions. He couldn't tell his team, or they'd refuse, and his wife would be killed. We're guessing they've taken all of them, apart from Steele, to the leaders of the cartel."

Dahl nodded. "Which cartel?"

Luther spoke first. "Ruiz."

Dahl grimaced. "Shit. Carlos Ruiz is one of the worst."

"Yeah, they're a bad bunch. They own an entire police force and most of the occupants of their closest town. Even when I worked for Tempest, they were considered untouchable."

"I guess you can see that in the amount of hardware they used and complete lack of respect for America they showed during the LA attack," Drake said.

Luther agreed. "Yeah, their leader, this Ruiz, thinks he's some kind of supreme being. Unchallenged. Better than everyone else. He has a major god complex."

"And men?" Dahl asked

"I can't remember the details," Luther said. "But he'll have an army, plus a police force."

"Well, Cara and the others clearly didn't know," Drake said. "You could see it on their faces. We can't just let them be taken by the bloody cartel."

Hayden slammed her phone against her leg. "It seems we can. Actually, it seems we've been ordered to."

Mai took a step forward. "I don't believe that. They're thieves but they're gonna get cut to pieces or forced into service. And the eggs? What kind of wealth will they bring to the cartel?"

"Mega," Drake said. "That's why they mounted this huge

operation in the first place. The wealth will be worth it."

"They're already super rich," Luther said.

"But only the second biggest cartel in Mexico. They want to be first. They want to be the biggest in the world, no doubt. Especially if this Ruiz is as arrogant as Luther says."

"He is."

Hayden held a hand up, stopping their conversation. "We're not allowed to pursue the cartel. Our government won't interfere. Ops are already years in the planning over there. The eggs are lost and we've been ordered to walk away."

"But one of the reasons we're here dovetails directly with those eggs," Karin said. "The unbelievable wealth their sale will drop on the market."

"Agreed," Hayden said, "but our boss, and his boss have ordered us to stand down."

Alicia stood impatiently, moving from foot to foot. Mai glanced at Drake and then Dahl. The team stared at the horizon or the sky or down at their boots, everyone running through the consequences of what they'd just heard.

Dahl caught Hayden's attention. "I think that's an extremely gray area."

Hayden fixed him with a glare. "Careful."

"Why? It's just us here. When we were SPEAR we answered to a boss, be it Special Forces, the Secretary of Defense or whoever. But now, we're on our own. And that was a deliberate act. We're not above the law, but the law doesn't technically rule us."

"You're saying we disobey orders?" Hayden sounded skeptical.

"Who controls us? The President. What's his view?"

"I don't know and I'm not gonna call him up right now."

Luther slapped Dahl on the back, a hard jolt that sent

dust billowing. "Good man," he said. "I say we go."

"Me too," Dahl said.

"Write our own ticket?" Alicia said. "Make our own decisions. That's what we do now? I'm good with that."

"You're all talking yourselves into as assault on a Mexican drug cartel that even the US government thinks is untouchable," Kinimaka said. "You know that, right?"

"The beauty of this new team," Mai said, "is exactly this. We're on our own. I say we go."

Hayden looked for the majority. She wasn't strictly the team leader any more. It would all be handled jointly unless they were in the thick of major battle, and then they'd defer to her. Nobody was abstaining. Everyone was electing to go.

Hayden looked over to the idling helicopters. "There's a ton of weapons lying around. Machine guns. Rocket launchers. Grenades. You name it, it's there, and we're gonna need all of it."

"Now that's what I'm talking about," Luther grinned. "Now we're back, boys and girls. Now we're back."

CHAPTER THIRTY FOUR

"Leave him alone! Please. He's had enough."

Cara's cry made the man called Ruiz pause. He turned to her, gazing steadily. He was an unspectacular man in every way. Mid-sized, black hair, black eyes. Middle aged. He seemed to support no muscle and no fat, he was just . . . ordinary.

Except he ran the second biggest and most dangerous cartel in the world.

Cara had never heard of him before today. She knew about the cartels and what they did, but had never taken time to learn about them. But none of that mattered now. She was here, inside his mansion in Mexico, guarded by his army of cutthroats, mercenaries and gunmen. There was no escape.

Alongside her, tied to chairs with thick ropes, were the rest of the One Percenters, and one other woman.

Jax's wife.

What a fucking shit show, she thought.

Ruiz stopped punching Jax for a moment to walk over. As he approached, Cara saw the ruthlessness in his face, the utter lack of anything regarding a soul. His mouth was a straight thin line and bore no crease lines, as if he'd never smiled and never frowned. He walked until he was uncomfortably close to her and she was staring at his chest.

"Pretty girl," he said. "I love your blond hair. I love the blood around your face and neck. I think that I will lick it off."

Cara somehow refrained from kicking out. She was a fighter. At school they'd bullied her for her good looks and skinny frame, but she'd overcome that and turned shame into confidence, fear into courage.

"You want to hit me. I can see it in your eyes," Ruiz said. "But it is good that you do not. I would rip those eyes out."

Cara swallowed and looked away. Ruiz not only appeared callous, but also superior, as if he owned not only this ranch but Mexico. To a point, Cara assumed that was true.

"He told you everything," she said. "I was alongside him the whole way. I know."

"He told me everything?" Ruiz repeated her and half-turned away, then spun his body back round, swinging with an open hand. The blow caught her across the face, snapping her head to the right. Cara blinked and tried to ignore the pain.

"Who are you? A piece of shit. You are nothing! I will kill you if you speak again."

Ruiz turned his back on her as if she was now dead to him but then half-turned. "You are sweet looking," he said. "I want to see how your blood tastes."

Cara shuddered as he walked away. She was courageous but this place was hell on earth. They'd been driven out of the desert, along an underground tunnel shored up by timbers, and into bright sunshine. Then they'd hit proper asphalt for the first time in hours, a welcome relief to her bruised and shaken bones.

Forty minutes later they were turning off the road, hitting more desert dunes, following a rudimentary path. Then, a shock to the senses. Ahead a striking mansion appeared, out here in the middle of a dry, dusty nowhere. It was surrounded by walls and guard towers and many gun-toting, rough-looking individuals. Jax had whispered that it was the cartel's HQ, their home, but she'd ignored him, hating him.

Now she wanted to save him.

Jax was tied to a wooden chair that had been bolted to the ground. His chest was bare. Ruiz had started out with a whip, an old-fashioned lasso. He'd gone onto pliers and had then donned a pair of leather gloves. Now, he was punching, sometimes kicking, asking Jax periodic questions in an attempt to confuse him.

If you were asked the same question a hundred times under duress and your answer never changed, it had to be the truth.

At least, that's what Cara imagined was happening. For all she knew Ruiz was just getting his morning tensions out of the way.

How did we get to this?

She'd had a rollercoaster life. From childhood troubles to street-life to brushes with the law and running with a wolf pack like the One Percenters. She'd honed her craft. Before this last job they never resorted to violence—even Steele had been tempered. Violence attracted violence and Cara wanted no part of it. Now she knew why Jax had gone off the rails. The reason sat three seats to her left.

Bella.

Apparently, that was her real name. Just Bella. She was Jax's secret wife, at least a secret from his own team. But from the Mexican cartel? Not so much. They'd kidnapped her and given Jax an ultimatum. Bring the eggs or receive her fingers, toes, hands . . .

The list had gone on and on with the cartel promising to keep her alive until the last possible moment. Her torture would have lasted months. Cara accepted that anyone that cared for a human being would have done exactly what Jax had done. But why hadn't he told her? They were experts at stealthy entry and exit for God's sake. Surely they could have rescued Bella together.

It would have been the job of legend.

But they'd never have been safe. Always looking over their shoulders for the cartel. Always worried. Life would have become a jittery hell.

And people like Kushner and Faye might not have wanted any part of it.

Cara saw Jax's reasoning. And why he'd resorted to violence. The stress on his ex-Marine shoulders would have been incredible, unbearable.

But it had all led them to this.

Ruiz now slid off his leather gloves and checked his knuckles. "Bruised," he said and then glared at Jax. "You bruised my knuckles."

Cara could barely stand to look at Jax. His left eye was closed, the skin around it starting to swell. His forehead and cheeks dripped blood and whenever he moved it ran freely from his mouth. Ruiz had dislodged several teeth. Jax's chest was crisscrossed with red stripes. His arms were a mass of cuts and bruises. He sagged in the chair, held in place only by the ropes that tied him to it.

Cara doubted he could speak now even if he wanted to. He'd already told Ruiz about the theft and the resulting chase. He'd told Ruiz that they were on their way to meet him on Venice Beach as planned.

"You were too slow," Ruiz had hissed, punching freely. "Late. I don't tolerate mistakes or delay. The only reason you're alive is because you called me on Venice Boulevard. I managed to rejig everything. Do you understand? It was me. Me that saved you, that stole the eggs, that saved all your lives. I am the mastermind here."

Cara closed her eyes when the beating had continued. There was nothing she could do. Her only hope was a peculiar one. The soldier she'd fallen next to in the desert—

the one who'd tried to save her life. Who'd jumped from the rock pile and run toward her, into the danger. She'd fallen at his side and whispered where they were bound.

That man was their only hope.

Cara wanted to cry. Her life had come to this. But that was just selfish and cowardly. She had to stay strong.

Now, Ruiz tilted Jax's face. "Open your eyes."

To his credit, Jax tried. The pain was evident. He managed to crack open one eyelid. "From now on, you work for me. You work for me for the rest of your life. You do what I say, when I say it." He spun. "And that goes for all of you. The One Percenters are now my property. Nod if you understand."

Cara nodded along with the others. Even Bella nodded. Ruiz looked satisfied. "You messed up the last job. Your first failure. Eight perfect heists and then one incredible fuck up. What happened?"

He turned toward Cara and the others, so she assumed it was safe to speak. "We were never a team," she said. "From the Fabergé job's start. It wasn't right between us."

"Are you blaming me?"

"Ah, no, no. I think it was Steele."

"You're blaming a corpse? Convenient. But I'm a fair man. I can see where he could have been a problem. My men told me what he was like."

Cara breathed out silently and slowly. It had been a gamble. But Ruiz wanted something and, hopefully, that was enough. If he sent them on future jobs, they would have the chance to talk and work out an escape strategy.

It was the single ray of light on a pitch-black horizon.

"You'll stay with me for a while," Ruiz said. "I want to . . . talk . . . to each of you separately. Like I talked to Jax. Then, after and if you recover, we'll look at another job."

Cara died inside a little. She faced a blasted, grim future. She swiveled her head to the left, looking at Faye, Kushner and Bella. Jax's wife was crying. Her face was swollen and bruised, as if she'd already been "talked to."

Kushner looked terrified. Even Faye, who'd never exhibited an ounce of emotion in the twelve years Cara had known her, looked scared out of her mind.

Ruiz took several steps toward them. "Who's next?" He grinned.

CHAPTER THIRTY FIVE

Drake enjoyed the smell of a safe house armory. It reminded him of army days long gone. Of good friends and good times. Of simpler days when an unknown, promising future stretched ahead of him, his to seize and mold. It was the same for every young person. The problem was, you never knew or wanted to know that until it was too late.

He stopped and looked around, nodding with satisfaction. "This'll do."

Kenzie squeezed by. "Me first."

Dahl was a millisecond after her. "Don't take all the good stuff."

Drake eyed the shelves. Since leaving the desert they'd researched Ruiz's property online, using a dedicated satellite, and found a safe approach. The satellite had been invaluable, pinpointing men, weapons movement, security systems, and much more. Just about every ounce of Intel they needed. And they had it for another four hours.

It wasn't legal. It didn't have a name. It was a CIA spying eye, one of many positioned over Mexico. The cartel assumed they operated in secrecy. The truth was that the CIA knew more about the cartel than their own citizens. Back in the desert, Hayden had taken a risk. They'd all wanted to continue with the mission despite the government's orders, reiterating that they were their own entity now.

They could act when and how they chose. It was part of the new agreement.

"But we can't just defy our directives," Hayden had said. "They're there for a reason. We could end up in jail."

"Directives?" Dahl had questioned. "Aren't they really guidelines?"

Hayden's expression had told them it was a gray area. They'd pushed ahead. With this mission being off book, Hayden had relented and called in several old favors. Kinimaka too. The CIA safe house just inside Mexico wasn't hard to appropriate. The satellite was.

Now, they both owed favors. And more. One of her old bosses in the CIA had made her promise the assistance of the entire Strike Force team if he ever needed it.

"That's a big ask," Hayden had said.

"It is what it is."

She'd checked and they'd agreed. Ten minutes later they had their own spy satellite.

Now, Drake pushed ahead into the armory, choosing reliable weapons. A HK and a Glock, various grenades and knives. He noticed Kenzie choose the biggest blade there, probably wishing it was a sword. Alicia chose wisely and so did the others. Soon, they backed out of the armory, returning to the main room.

Karin was seated at a low table, leaning over a big laptop. She was using the satellite to zoom in on various parts of Ruiz's property, highlighting security measures and trying to get a handle on movement.

"See here," she said as she sensed their return. "Underground rooms. A bunker. A wine cellar. And tunnels, here and here. Escape tunnels, probably. All the cartel bosses have them."

"Can we use the tunnels?" Dahl asked.

"It's the only point of entry we can use," Karin said. "But it means we'll have the full force of the cartel bearing down once they spot us."

"Some help would be useful," Mai said.

"You know what Cooper and those other guys said. We're on our own. We're mercenaries now, not agents."

Alicia sniffed. "Does that mean I suddenly have a lower IQ?"

"Hey, not all mercs are knuckleheads. Many are just like you."

Mai and Kenzie both winced. "God help them."

Alicia nodded in agreement. "No argument there."

Dahl tapped the screen. "Where are we with the security system?"

"I have a remote jamming tool. I have a way to spoof and loop the feed thanks to Langley. We can knock out their sensors with a few shenanigans. False alarms. We can draw men away from the house to check the grounds using distraction techniques. I've come up with three already. But . . . we can't be seen. If we're seen we're in the battle of our lives."

"Any sign of the eggs?" Dallas asked, a question that struck Drake quite poignantly. It was a question that Yorgi would ask, and he wished the young Russian thief was with them.

"I pinpointed three safes. One big iron mother and two normal sized. Unfortunately, the eggs aren't fitted with any trackers I can see. Maybe the One Percenters rigged something. We can ask them when we find them, but . . ."

"We know," Drake said. "We can't risk being seen."

"Anything else?" Luther asked, big fingers gripping his gun.

"The tunnels run straight into the wine cellar. After that it's the rooms, which could be cells, maybe an armory. There're two sets of stairs leading out of there, so two points of ingress to cover. I'm guessing we'll be moving fast so will need something special waiting outside to assure a quick getaway."

Dahl looked at Drake and shook his head. "A Lambo's not gonna cut it," he said. "So get that right out of your head."

"No car," Karin said. "The cartel has helicopters as we know. Even planes. When I said special, I meant it."

"How many of us will there be?" Luther asked cautiously. "I may be able to call in a favor of my own."

Karin counted it in her head. "Sixteen," she said. "But who knows? Allow for two more."

Luther glanced over at Molokai. "What do you think?"

"Yeah, could be done." Clearly, they were both on the same wavelength.

"Seventeen?"

"It's fine. We'll have to man the weapons though."

"What are you two talking about?" Kinimaka asked.

"Don't worry," Luther smiled. "Just call it exfil sorted."

"I do worry," Hayden said.

"There's an army base in San Diego. If I shout loud enough, and call in every favor, I can get us a big bird."

Mai pushed her way in. "The tunnels," she said. "Where do they begin?"

Karin pointed to a range of hills about two miles from Ruiz's mansion. It was clear that they were to the northeast of the house's position, closer to the American border. Interestingly, Ruiz thought his best escape route was closer to his apparent enemy and attacker.

"We can chopper in a few miles north," Karin said. "That's plenty far enough from the house."

"So we're ready?" Dallas asked.

Kenzie nodded. "You sound excited?"

"I still have something to prove."

Drake was reminded that they hadn't properly screened this guy yet. Once they split up after the Devil's Island mission all thoughts of work had purposely been put on hold. It had been rest and recuperation, sand, sex and cocktails. Not in that order or frequency.

Weirdly, he was glad to be right here, right now. Back in the field.

"You know," he said aloud. "I'm not sure I could take another three-month layoff."

Almost everyone smiled and nodded in agreement. Molokai made a point of tapping Hayden on the shoulder. "Take more jobs," he said. "It doesn't matter too much what they are. We're capable of anything."

Drake noted the only ones not in full agreement were the new couples. Mai and Luther. Karin and Dino. Even Hayden and Kinimaka looked dubious.

"We should probably shelve this for another day," he said. "Tool up and head out."

"When my kids leave," Dahl said. "I will probably have to take a few jobs."

Drake paused, halfway across the room. He looked back at the Swede and saw an unguarded anguish in his face. "I'll go with you," he said.

"And me," Alicia added.

Dahl smiled at her. "You still running for that horizon?"

"Only when I have to or when my friends need me to."

Mai had always been loyal to the team. "Just call me," she said. "I'll be there."

Hayden grabbed a bottle of water from the fridge. "I'm positive there will be something, even if we have to force it."

"Force it?" Dahl wondered.

"I'll get us something," she said.

Everyone agreed. Kinimaka drifted closer to the big Swede, almost as if he felt the need to protect him in that moment as he often did Hayden. Luther said he'd go anywhere with Mai, which raised several eyebrows, including Molokai's.

For a moment Drake thought he'd seen a rare flash of amusement on the robed man's face.

Kenzie rose and walked over to Dahl, staring him right in the eyes. All movement in the room stopped.

"Whatever happened before doesn't matter," she said. "When you need me . . ."

She let it hang. Drake wondered at her choice of words. When? Not if?

Finally, Dahl nodded at them and turned away, finishing his preparations. Drake reflected over all that had happened during the last three months. The Caribbean getaway, the awkward reintroduction to civilian life. The first vacation week had been spent scanning for enemies, wondering if the waiters were spiking drinks or carrying hidden firearms. A quiet, peaceful ambiance just didn't suit him.

Or Alicia.

"I'm happy with the new team and writing our own ticket," he said. "But I agree, we shouldn't wait three months next time for some action."

Alicia nodded firmly. "God, yeah. Drake's more boring than a priest at a hooker convention."

He turned hurt eyes on her. "Well, thanks, love."

"Do you think they have those?" Kinimaka asked without thinking. "Hooker conventions?"

Hayden stopped and turned to him. "Why do you ask?"

"No reason. Just wondering." Kinimaka turned away to hide a grin at his own foolishness.

Drake stopped at the door, turned and looked over the large crew, ready to go out and do war, to risk their lives for no reward. The eggs were simply art and the One

Percenters were criminals. It was a rare, selfless group he worked with.

"I missed you guys," he said.

They headed out the door.

CHAPTER THIRTY SIX

They were utterly silent; predators in the night, creeping toward their prey. Blackness shrouded them like a cloak, as if welcoming their presence. Despite their gear, the amount of weaponry they carried, they were ghosts.

Drake slipped night-vision goggles over his eyes, and approached the range of hills in which the tunnel entrance lay. They'd pinpointed it by satellite and were now closing in on the precise location on foot. Comms were active.

"Two guards," Drake whispered. "Waiting five as agreed. Checking for radios."

The cartel had owned this area for a long time. They didn't expect unannounced visitors. The guards were just a token presence, possibly even sent out here as some kind of punishment, to do a job that didn't really need doing.

"Looks clear," Karin said. "I'm detecting no radio frequencies."

They'd brought a good array of up-to-date tech with them.

Drake started to move. Dahl rushed past him, silenced MP5 submachine gun at the ready. He'd finally gone for compact and lightweight, but retained the ability to do damage at close or far range. The MP5 was incredibly versatile. Luther was a step behind the Swede. Drake let them go. Dahl crept up on the blind side of the two guards, lined them up and fired four times.

Drake saw two figures roll lifelessly down the slope.

Luther was covering, just in case Dahl missed a shot. Now, he eased out of hiding and crept over to the spot the two men had been guarding.

"Clear," he reported through the comms.

Drake came around to take a look. Barely discernible in the dark was a ragged entrance cut into the hillside. It was sealed by a wooden door, overhung with greenery and surrounded by rocks.

"It's a good job we had the human markers," Mai said. "We'd never have found it."

Drake smiled. It was curious to see what great planning and good luck threw back at you. Kinimaka and Hayden tugged at the door. They weren't surprised to see it open easily and smoothly.

"Escape route," Karin said by way of explanation. "Not to be neglected."

They entered the tunnel slowly, using their night-vision at first, but then breaking out the flashlights. It was totally dark down here. Drake shone his flashlight around, picking out earthy, shored-up tunnels, an uneven, rock-strewn floor and a string of lights attached to the roof above. It was definitely makeshift, but it would work.

"I wonder how they'd finish their getaway," Kinimaka asked. "Once outside, I mean."

"Same way we are," Luther said. "In style."

Drake recalled they still didn't know Luther's exact plan, but he trusted the man. If his support in battle wasn't enough, Mai's faith certainly was.

The tunnel stretched ahead, dark and straight and getting gradually deeper. Karin had a device that counted the steps and monitored how close to their goal they were getting. Luther and Dahl ranged ahead at first, checking for guards that weren't expected, then swopped with Dallas and Dino, the two relative newcomers eager to take the lead.

"Buckle up now," Karin said. "We're approaching the tunnel's end."

Drake eased the tension out of his shoulders. A few minutes later they came up against a second door, this one locked from the other side.

Alicia swore. "I didn't expect that. Did we expect that?"

Karin nodded. "I did."

Quickly, she mixed two small vials of chemicals and poured the resulting substance on the door handle. The hard metal melted within two minutes and began to pour down the door. Kinimaka found he could just nudge the wooden panel.

"Ready," he said.

It opened inward. Drake went third, finding himself inside another tunnel, this one far better constructed. It had a high ceiling and proper rafters, sturdy supports with iron braces and a concrete floor. It was well-lit too.

Drake checked for cameras. "Clear."

It was a short way to the next door. Karin stopped them for a moment.

"Past here, we're in the wine cellar. Beyond that are the underground cells, we believe. There are four prisoners that we definitely know about. And there are the eggs."

"Let's get it done." Dahl pushed at the door, which was locked, and waited for Karin to do her thing with the chemicals. The door opened inward. Drake was treated to the sight of hundreds of dusty wooden shelves to each side, filled with bottles of wine. The first aisle stretched for about thirty feet.

Dahl went first. Drake followed. They progressed silently down the first aisle, senses attuned. They were underneath the main house now which, they guessed, was guarded by roughly one hundred men. Drake reached the end of the aisle and looked left. He could see the far side of the wine cellar and an arched opening that led to the cells. Staring hard, he could make out several sets of bars.

"Looks like we were right."

From behind there came a clink. Drake, and everyone behind him, looked back, weapons raised.

Kinimaka was pulling two bottles off the shelves. When he looked up he started, seeing he was under scrutiny. He shrugged. "Hey, it doesn't matter if you're visiting the cartel's cellar or the Queen of England's. If there's good bottles of wine down there you make sure they're in your backpack when you leave."

Kenzie nodded her agreement. "That's a good point." She thrust a couple of the dusty bottles into her own pack.

Drake gestured unhappily. "Are we ready now?"

"Just waiting for you."

Drake took the long walk to the far side of the wine cellar alone, checking every aisle. When he reached the archway, he stopped and checked inside.

"Guard room," he said. "They're playing cards. I see four."

"Cells?" Hayden asked.

"Yeah, at least a dozen. Can't see any occupants."

He waited, allowing the tension to seep out of his body. The rest of the team joined him. The guard room was to the right and the door was wide open.

They moved, Drake and Dahl first. The walls, ceiling and floor were all hewn out of rock. Their footsteps were silent. Luther and Molokai backed them up whilst the others waited, not wanting to venture further inside in case an inmate shouted out.

Drake fired, shooting one man through the head and chest. Dahl did the same. They ran inside the room. A third man was reaching for a gun that was propped up against the table leg. Drake shot him twice in the back of the head and neck. The last man managed to lift his handgun off the table and raise it before Dahl ended his life.

Drake checked the rest of the room. It was small, consisting of a refrigerator, a bar for bottles of liquor and a coffee maker and a bin. The dead men stared back at him in their various positions of repose, seeing nothing. He turned and walked out.

"Go," he said through the comms.

Hayden led the others through the cell cave. Six stood to either side, thick metal bars running floor to ceiling. They took them two at a time, training their guns through the bars. Once they reached the end they turned back around.

"Five people," Hayden said.

Shouts were already coming from the cells. Drake saw Cara's blond hair appear, her hands gripping the bars. He saw Jax and two more figures. Two voices were loud, but the others were hushed. They'd already suffered down here.

Drake stuck to the plan. They didn't have a lot of time to waste, but hadn't been spotted yet, so weren't under too much pressure.

Hayden supervised the opening of doors. The remaining four members of the One Percenters and another woman walked or stumbled out, looking wary. Hayden wasted no time telling them what was going to happen.

"You're not free and you're definitely not safe. Thanks to you guys we now have to go upstairs and retrieve those eggs you stole. You'll wait here, under guard, until we get back. Understood?"

Dallas and Dino stepped forward, one guard each for two One Percenters, with guns aimed to show they meant what they said.

"No bullshit. No escape attempts. You keep it down or we leave you here. Got it?"

Cara nodded for all of them, seeking Drake out with her eyes. "Thank you," she said.

The Yorkshireman nodded. "Just stay calm. We won't be long."

"You . . . should . . . leave those fucking eggs behind," Jax faltered, hanging on to one of the bars to keep himself upright. "Brought me nothing but trouble."

The unknown woman ran at Jax, grabbing him under a shoulder and hefting him up. She was crying, sobbing. She brushed Jax's face and tried to shore him up.

"I . . . I'm okay love," he said.

"That's it?" Dahl asked. "They kidnapped your wife?"

"Yeah, you would do the same."

"I don't doubt it."

Cara scowled at the ground. "But you should have told us."

Jax leaned on his wife's shoulder. "You know I couldn't. Kushner at least would have refused, and we couldn't have pulled it off without him."

Kushner didn't protest. He was staring at the roof and the walls as if seeking a way out, ignoring proceedings.

Cara looked betrayed. "We would have found a way."

"Quick question," Hayden said. "Did you guys put any kind of tracker on the eggs? Anything to make it easier to find them."

"I told you we should have," Cara told Jax.

"No," Jax said. "She's right, but I couldn't risk the cartel finding the tracker and using that as an excuse to hurt Bella."

Dahl scratched an ear. "You really think they need an excuse? You think they were gonna let you go?"

"Not even close," Cara said. "We were about to become their new puppets. They pull one string we rob a place in the US. They pull another we head to Eastern Europe. You understand?"

Drake nodded, disappointed but not shocked. It was then that Faye spoke up in a quiet, breathy voice. "I'm sorry," she said to Jax. "But I did put a tracker in them. At least, in one of the boxes."

Jax closed his eyes and shook his head, then glanced at Cara. "And you wonder why I didn't tell anyone about Bella?"

"I helped make the boxes," Faye said. "I inserted a small bug inside the machine-tooled foam we created to house the eggs according to online dimensions. The tracker's so small you won't spot it and had a redundancy of one day. It should have started working now."

Karin conferred with Faye about the tracker's frequency. Soon, she had a flashing green dot on her mobile tablet. "Got it."

Drake stepped forward. "Hey, I'm happy for you guys to chat. Get your feelings out in the open. But these two will perforate you if you make any stupid moves, and you need to get him ready to move fast when we return."

He nodded at Jax. Cara and Faye walked over to him. Dallas and Dino moved to cover them.

Drake pressed his comms. "Everyone else. Let's go kick some cartel arse."

CHAPTER THIRTY SEVEN

They returned to the wine cellar, found a set of stairs and climbed them to the house's ground floor. Faye's flashing green dot told them the eggs and, presumably, the big iron safe or some kind of vault, were one floor up. Drake paused at the top of the stairs to give everyone time to make ready.

Then he pushed hard, and they were out. No more finesse or silence. They entered a kitchen, wide and spacious and mostly white. Three men stood inside. Drake opened fire, killing one that stood by a counter eating a sandwich. Luther wasted a second, catching him by the open fridge, tipping half a pint of milk down his throat.

The third was just too close.

He was right in front of Drake, shock stretching his features, but he wasn't slow and drew a handgun in an instant. Drake leapt at him, driving him back to the wall. The gun discharged, the bullet passing under Drake's shoulder and hitting the door jamb next to Dahl's head. The Swede muttered a curse, moved to Drake and shot the guard through the temple.

Drake spun and exited the kitchen. Luther was ahead of him, followed by Hayden. They fired, catching two guards with three rounds. They entered a study, lined with bookcases and old paintings. An old desk stood to the left and a huge globe to the right. The room was empty. Luther ran through it, staying low. He followed a blinking map attached to a mini-tablet on his left wrist, heading for the nearest staircase. Drake checked to left and right. They exited the study and came to an expansive living room.

"Nine marks," Luther muttered.

Drake ran fast, joining Luther and the others as they surged into the living room. Shots popped off, the sound muffled by the big silencers. The Mexicans fell backward, blood spraying the couch and the walls. Alicia and Mai came in fast, choosing other targets. One man dived headlong to the ground, pulling out a handgun as he went. He fired back, the shots flying wide. Another enemy returned fire, but he was in panic, the bullets riddling the roof eight feet above Drake's head.

Strike Force One spread out, fanning through the room. Drake took out two men hiding behind the sofa, not sure how they thought it would protect them. They all ducked when several rounds of more purposeful fire came from the far side of the room. But this had to be a fluid op. They couldn't afford to stop moving and get pinned down.

Mai threw her flash-bang grenade. It stunned the shooter, enabling Hayden and Kinimaka to rush him and end his life. The team pushed through a far door, into the house's front lobby—a wide, high, white-painted vestibule, the space larger than many houses Drake had seen.

To their left, a wide staircase wound up to higher floors. On the right, a pair of wide front doors were partially open. Beside them, a row of glass windows looked out onto the expansive gardens. They could see the entire front lawn.

Dahl headed for the staircase. "Safe is less than two minutes away."

Drake looked at Alicia. "Make some fucking noise."

Alicia grinned. She removed her silencer and held a finger down on her weapon's trigger, spraying the whole front façade and breaking every window. Not only were the gunshots loud but the sound of shattering glass would be heard for about half a mile.

They all had to work seamlessly now.

Dahl led the way up. Cartel guards were coming down the staircase. Dahl and Luther picked them off, firing through the staircase balustrade, their guns poking through the finely wrought spindles.

Dead men collapsed down the stairs, falling freely. Dahl stepped over them. Drake and Karin followed the Swede and Luther up front.

But they were on their own.

The rest of the team had stayed below, leaving those on the stairs and rushing into another room, out of sight.

"Here they come," Kenzie cried out through the comms.

"How many?" Drake asked.

"A fuckload!"

Assuming she meant more than one and less than a hundred, Drake pounded up the bare wood stairs. There were shouts from below, cursing and challenges as cartel soldiers saw them and gave chase. Shots rang out at the same time, following the team all the way up to the next floor. Drake managed one quick glance down.

The huge lobby was rapidly being filled by Mexicans carrying an assortment of weapons. They seemed unsure at the moment, as if lacking leadership. Some stood whilst others took pot shots, but none ran at the stairs. Drake counted thirty men as someone shouted.

"They're about to give chase," he said.

"Do we have enough time?" Dahl asked Karin.

"No. Make us some more."

She raced ahead with Luther. Dahl stopped and spun, dropping to one knee and resting the MP5 over his right shoulder. "You with me, Drake?"

"Always, mate."

Dahl glanced at him with suspicion. "Always?"

"Always in battle."

"That's okay then."

They laid down the lead as cartel guards steamed up the winding staircase. Wooden spindles, banisters and newel posts shattered and splintered as bullets slammed through. Guards twisted, yelled and died, slithering back down the risers and tripping their colleagues. Others dived headlong, trying to hide amid the wood and dead bodies.

The lobby was full now, dozens of men were down there. Many fired back up, destroying the top of the staircase and pulverizing the plaster wall to the right of Drake and Dahl with bullets.

"Who is that? Who attacks my house?" The voice was loud, guttural and manic.

Drake saw an opportunity to give Karin more time. "Who the hell are you?"

There were many gasps, but then his question was answered. "I am Ruiz. I own this fucking country."

"That's not quite true," Dahl called back. "At least not until we leave."

Ruiz cursed him. "English? What are the fucking English doing here?"

"We just came to party, Roo," Drake drawled.

"You got foxes in the henhouse, Roo." Dahl grinned. "Stealing your eggs."

Ruiz's stentorian cry filled the lobby. "Stop those motherfuckers!"

Drake turned to Dahl. "Did he just call us mothercluckers?"

They opened fire, taking down several more men. But far more were surging up. Drake knew they now faced the bulk of Ruiz's force.

Perfect.

They turned and ran. Drake keyed the comms. "We're coming in hot, ready or not."

"Thirty seconds."

"Fuck, we don't have thirty seconds."

But Dahl was turning his body on the run, looking backward and plucking a grenade from his belt. He hurled it underhand so that it bounced at the top of the stairs, then bumped its way down, riser by riser.

Right into the upcoming men.

The explosion boomed out seconds later. Cartel guards flew against the hard wall or over the edge of the staircase, falling among those still below. Pandemonium reigned. Drake fired several more rounds of ammo to back up the grenade and then continued the run.

Together, they burst into the room where the safe was situated.

Karin was on her knees. Luther to the right, covering their door and another that stood at his back. Two men lay dead near his feet.

"Where are we?" Dahl cried.

"Almost . . . there . . ."

The sounds of pursuit came down the hallway behind them.

"This is too fucking close," Drake said.

Nevertheless, for their plan to work everything had to happen at the same time. Karin gave them the thumbs up. Luther turned and ran for the far door. Karin rose to her feet as Drake and Dahl reached her.

"All good?"

"I hope so."

Drake glanced at the enormous iron safe. It stood to their left, away from the wall, about five feet high and three feet wide. It was old, it was protected by a tumbler lock, and it was sturdy. The front door was covered in ornate patterns.

"No time," Dahl said, still running.

Drake pushed Karin ahead of him, then turned as the door they'd entered by was strafed by bullets. Three seconds later men charged into the safe room.

Drake and Dahl were on their knees by the far door, firing.

Bullets riddled their enemies, striking legs and chests and heads, but many more pressed in behind them. Drake waited as long as he could. Dahl waited two seconds later. They fired to draw their enemy inside, backed away and watched the surge of men start to give chase. Dozens were pouring into the safe room; the bulk of Ruiz's men.

Drake flung himself to the floor.

Dahl cried, "Now!"

Karin depressed a button. The explosive charge she'd placed around the safe and the floor area detonated with a devastating crack of thunder. The men in the room never knew what hit them. Fire filled the room, debris discharged so fast it broke human bone and pierced bodies.

The entire floor caved in.

The huge safe fell through to the floor below, along with dozens of men. Some were still entering the safe room, some were already dead, but many were alive as they fell with the shattered floor, impacting hard twenty feet below. Shards of timber and chunks of plaster fell with them.

The rest of the Strike Force team were waiting below to finish off any survivors.

Gunfire rang out. Drake and Dahl rose and ran to the edge of the devastated floor. They peered down as Luther watched ahead in case anyone tried to enter through the demolished door.

The safe had landed hard, its sides bowed, its front melted, its tumbler burned away by the intensely hot explosive flare Karin had used to destroy it. The flare had been localized, and facing away so as not to harm the safe's contents. The fall had been judged short enough to shake the contents but not damage them. They couldn't hope for much more considering the circumstances. Drake saw many bodies down there, twisted and broken, their firearms still clutched in their fingers or lying beside them.

When it's kill or be killed, perhaps tortured too, you don't fuck about.

Dahl stepped forward. "We doing this, or what?"

They unhooked ropes from the sides of their backpacks, looped it around exposed timbers and let it unfurl to the floor below. Drake radioed in that they were on their way down. Hayden told them to wait a few seconds as they dealt with some survivors.

"What's the situation?" Luther asked.

"There are dozens in the lobby. We still have a fight on our hands."

"Ruiz?"

"Yeah, cockroaches don't die easily."

Dahl jumped onto a rope and let himself down. Drake followed suit. Soon they stood among the debris and the dead men. To his right, Kenzie, Kinimaka and Mai were emptying the safe of the Fabergé eggs and stuffing them into spare packs. The door that led to the lobby had collapsed, giving them a little respite.

"We good?" Dahl looked around.

"Yeah, we're ready," Mai said.

"Back to the wine cellar," Kinimaka said, not without some relish in his voice.

Drake looked to Hayden and Karin. "Is there a route past them . . . or . . ."

"No, mate," Dahl smiled, "We're going through them. You know it makes sense."

CHAPTER THIRTY EIGHT

Karin's blueprints, taken from the borrowed CIA satellite, proved invaluable. Life-saving. They packed the eggs away and left the room via a rear door, moving deeper into the house. Another large area was navigated and then a cinema room where a big-screen projector stood among pool tables. The heavy sound of pursuit followed them. Ruiz couldn't seem to stop yelling.

"That is one angry man," Mai said at one point.

"Yeah, anyone would think we destroyed half his home," Hayden said.

Dahl rolled another grenade in their wake. "I enjoy hearing him scream."

The explosion rocked the house, taking down another wall and hindering Ruiz's men. Karin led the way, guarded by Luther and Kinimaka, to the very rear of the house. She was about to reach out and open the back door, but Dahl and Drake destroyed it with bullets.

"Sorry," the Yorkshireman said. "Couldn't help it."

They ran out into the night, breathing warm air. A breeze was blowing. Out here, spotlights lit up the rear grounds, shining on the enormous grill area, the Olympic size pool, a landscaped rock arrangement and countless palm trees. Clouds scudded across a starry, silvery sky lit by a three-quarter moon.

Karin indicated the way. Drake glanced backward. There were no signs of pursuit, but he could hear them. At a guess, they'd gained themselves a minute at the most.

Not long enough to return to the cell area and then go back to the wine cellar where the escape tunnel was situated.

"I'm thinking we need to engineer another thirty seconds," he told Dahl.

The Swede grinned. "Now you're talking."

Together, they rigged a simple trap. They rolled debris in their path, anchored the pins of two grenades to some of the sturdier rubble and buried them underneath it all. When the men waded through it, they'd trigger the bombs.

Dahl also threw two smoke grenades, obscuring the entire area.

It had to be enough. They sprinted off in pursuit of their team and caught up just as Karin came to the edge of the house.

"Forty feet down here—" she pointed along the eastern wall "—is a side door back to the kitchen."

The team readied themselves. Four cartel men were stalking along the wall, possibly trying to sneak up on them from the back but they were moving way too slow. Hayden and Luther leapt out, aimed and took them down, backed up by the rest of the team. Then they ran.

With a landscaped grass incline topped by trees to their right, they hugged the wall of the house and gained the side door. At that point there came a loud whump as their grenades exploded, causing more chaos among Ruiz's men. Then they were inside again, recognizing the bright white walls of the kitchen.

Hayden ran for the wine cellar door. Immediately, they heard gunshots echoing from below.

"Ruiz must have sent men for the One Percenters," Hayden said. "Hurry."

It had been one of their chief concerns. They'd hoped Ruiz would be too incensed to remember the thieves as he chased the eggs, but the gamble hadn't paid off. Speeding up to full pace, they dashed down the stairs and into the wine cellar, conscious they only had a ninety-second head start and that there were gunmen ahead of them.

Drake and Dahl spread out among the narrow aisles, wine bottles to both sides. The shelves reached high above them. The entire team took separate aisles as they approached the gunfire.

Drake peered out first. To the left, he saw the backs of four men, in hiding, peeking out occasionally and sending bullets toward the cell area, where Dallas and Dino crouched, firing back. Two Mexicans were already dead.

Drake could hear Cara shouting for a gun to defend herself. He was thinking that wouldn't be a good idea when he saw Dallas throw one to her. The weapon arced from one side of the room to the other. A Mexican tried to shoot it but missed. Drake frowned.

"Move," he said.

They burst from shelter. Bullets tagged the four Mexicans in their backs, from head to base of the spine. They fell forward, dead. Drake shouted at Dallas and Dino.

"You have ninety seconds. Get down here!"

Dallas herded Faye and Kushner to the center. Dino helped Jax along, followed by the man's wife. As Drake and Dahl ran forward, they saw Cara leveling the handgun at Dino.

"I can't go to prison."

"We don't have time for this," Drake hissed the words at her. "There's thirty heavily armed men about sixty seconds away."

"And the local army," Dahl added. "Let's not forget he'll have called them."

"Shit, I did forget." Drake turned to Dahl.

"Hey! I told you to let us go," Cara cried, stepping forward.

Drake whirled, grabbed the blonde's wrist and yanked it hard. She screamed, letting go of the gun. Alicia shouted from behind.

"Stop with the fucking foreplay will you. We've a big chopper to jump on."

"My big chopper," Luther said, but his grin froze when Mai sent him a look that would crush granite.

Dahl picked up the gun. Drake dragged Cara into the wine cellar and told her to behave. In seconds, everyone was ready.

"One last sprint up the tunnels," Drake said. "And we're clear."

"Almost," Luther said, "if my boys made it."

"If?"

As one, the team hurried along the length of the wine cellar and then switched right, racing down the aisles between dusty wooden shelves and vintage bottles. Kinimaka couldn't tear his eyes away from the endless display of bottles and Kenzie, at his back, was almost as entranced. They weren't even halfway down the aisle when they heard men pounding down the stairs.

Drake cursed inwardly. It wasn't enough time. Barely twenty seconds. They'd be picked off in the tunnels or even outside as they tried to board the getaway vehicle. A surge of anger swept through him. If they hadn't had to stop for the One Percenters. If Cara hadn't . . .

"Run!" Dahl shouted at their backs.

Cartel guards jumped down the steps in their dozens, guns waving and, in some cases, firing at the ceiling. Ruiz was among them, instantly seeing the runners.

"Kill them all!" Ruiz shrieked.

It was a desperate moment. They couldn't stop and risk being pinned down here. The stairs overlooked their position. More Mexicans were approaching the aisles. Hayden, at the front, entered the tunnel, followed by Dallas, Dino and the One Percenters, Kinimaka and Molokai.

But the rest of the team were still in the aisles. They were sitting ducks.

Drake turned, still running, firing shots in his wake. Bullets slammed past him, skimming uncomfortably close. Ahead, Kinimaka stopped dead and turned, gun shouldered, weapon on full-auto.

"God forgive me!" he cried.

The Hawaiian decimated the wine shelves with bullets. Shelves sagged and shattered. Bottles leapt into the air and sprayed red everywhere. The sound was tremendous. Drake and the others turned and ran hard as Kinimaka laid waste in their wakes.

Broken shelves full of bottles sagged and surged across the cellar floor, filling it. Wine drenched the cellar. Shelves folded on top of shelves collapsing heavily and loudly. Kenzie looked like she was about to cry at the Hawaiian's side.

"Fuck, Mano, I don't think I can forgive you for this."

"That's okay. I doubt I'll ever forgive myself."

Drake was clear, entering the long tunnel. Kinimaka and Kenzie spun and ran at his back as bullets thudded into the walls behind them. They were in the pitch black now, their way marked only by the swaying flashlights of their companions. The earthen walls suffocated sound, making it hard to discern how close their pursuers were. Drake knew it wouldn't take the cartel long to wade through the broken shelving.

The tunnel stretched ahead. The only sound was their panting and the occasional curse as one of them smacked against a wooden stanchion. It had crossed Drake's mind to use grenades to block the tunnel behind them, but they couldn't be entirely sure it wouldn't bring the whole system down.

To cast doubt in their pursuers' minds, he turned and unleashed a salvo of lead, then continued sprinting.

Hayden came on the comms. "Nearing the exit."

Drake saw flashlights starting to merge ahead, throwing a steady glow over what was happening at the entrance. Hayden and Luther emerged first, carefully, in case Ruiz had the foresight to send men around. He hadn't. Soon, Molokai was out, turning and pulling the One Percenters after him.

Luther ran to the front of the pack.

The big man took out his cellphone, which contained a navigation app, and signed in. A second later he looked off to the right.

"They're here. Waiting for us."

Drake pushed out into the night. "Move, guys, we're just a few minutes ahead."

They ran down the hillsides, slipping and sliding on gravel. The night air caressed their faces, the cool breeze drying their sweat. Drake cast from side to side but saw no movement. They moved as a team; the leaders forging ahead whilst Dino and Dallas guarded their captives; the others ranging to the sides and the rear for cover. Nothing would get by them.

"How far?" Hayden asked.

"Four klicks," Luther said.

"What's that in Yorkshire?" Alicia was next to Drake.

He shook his head at her. "Don't you remember your training? About two miles."

"I remember the instructor," she said with a roguish grin.

They reached the bottom of the hill and ran up the next. The terrain was sandy, full of boulders and rocky outcroppings. The only cover was the endless mounds and stony hillocks that stretched for miles. To the far right, Drake could make out Ruiz's home, marked by lights, smoke and fire.

Something reoccurred to him then, something he'd mentioned earlier to the team at large. The cartel never forgave, and they never stopped looking. They'd never let this drop. Even the One Percenters, despite the fact that they'd been rescued, would be high-value targets. Of course, the cartel didn't know the identities of the Strike Force.

It was a moot point. The op was ongoing. They'd devastated the cartel on their own turf. Drake set his mind straight and focused on the getaway. Shouting erupted from behind. He turned to see dozens of men emerging from the tunnel entrance.

"Cover," he cried.

Shots rang out. Bullets fired from handgun and machine guns flew wide and high. The team dived to the ground, but continued to scuttle ahead, staying low. They were halfway to their exfil point.

Drake stopped, turned, and opened fire. Alicia and Mai were with him. It served to send their pursuers running for cover and gain them more time. Minutes passed this way—an exchange of gunfire and then a mad dash until Ruiz appeared behind them.

Drake heard him screaming, but only caught a few words.

"Stop hiding and . . . them now! Or I'll . . ."

The impact of his words was clear. About twenty five Mexicans and Ruiz rushed after them in a group, reckless and unprotected, laying down constant fire. Drake and the others hit the top of a rock mound and then rushed down into a wide valley, temporarily shielded from the bullets.

Ahead, they saw a stunning and welcome sight.

Thunder filled the valley, as did Luther's getaway vehicle.

CHAPTER THIRTY NINE

It was a light gray, CH-53K King Stallion; the most powerful, modern and smartest helicopter that the United States military had ever seen. Twenty eight feet high and a hundred feet long, it could travel at 230mph. One of its key roles was to evacuate personnel from hot military and ongoing disaster zones and, to facilitate this, it had window and ramp mounted machine guns.

Its rear ramp was down, and its cutting-edge composite rotors were spinning fast, allowing it to rise slowly from the ground as first Hayden and then the rest of the Strike Force team ran hard toward it.

They ate up the ground fast, but not fast enough.

Ruiz and his men soon topped the last rocky rise and saw what waited for the escapees. The King Stallion was lit, loud and hugely impressive, but it didn't stop the Mexicans from firing their handguns at it.

"The soldiers!" Ruiz shouted. "Shoot the soldiers!"

Drake dived and rolled, coming up facing backward, firing several volleys. Bullets kicked up dust and gravel around the Mexicans. Some charged down the slope, others took aim. Drake and Dahl and Mai formed a rearguard, covering their friends. Marines ran down the helicopter's rear ramp, ready to reinforce the team. Gunfire blasted back and forth across the valley.

Ruiz advanced steadily, clearly unable to see defeat or the prudence of retreat. *Gods, it seemed, don't back down,* Drake thought. *Because they're invincible, right?*

He, Dahl and Mai backed away to the big Sikorsky. The rest of their team were on the ramp, laying down covering fire and, when he looked, back, Drake's heart missed a beat. It was an awesome sight. The Strike Force team and the Marines together in three rows; front row lying down, second row kneeling, third row standing and sending unstoppable, lethal hails of firepower right across the valley and straight into the heart of Ruiz's brutal cartel.

Drake choked up a little. It was one of the greatest sights of his life. This was living. This was reality. This was friendship. This was everything he'd ever wanted; not eating pizza and lounging on a beach. The heart of battle was Drake's home.

He ran among them and they were safe and free. Hayden radioed the pilots. The Sikorsky lifted higher, rotors chopping in relentless succession. The chopper's incredible thunder was deafening. The back end lifted just as the front end spun around.

"One more gift we've arranged for Ruiz," Luther said.

Three fifty-caliber machine guns were aimed at the remaining members of the cartel.

Drake backed up the ramp as the horizon wobbled. He could see Ruiz still shouting at his men, still berating and threatening them, even as the fifty cals focused on him.

"Goodnight, motherfucker," he whispered.

It looked and sounded like the whole area had exploded when the machine guns opened fire. The rocky hillside where the cartel stood shattered apart as the massive shells impacted. Men were shredded. Ruiz was lost in a cloud of blood that blended with all the rock dust and body parts to rain down as a thick red miasma. The guns didn't stop until everything stopped moving and then the sound of silence was almost deafening.

The Sikorsky hovered. Drake watched the dust settle. Nothing moved down there anymore, not rock, not flesh and bone, not sand. It was still, the fresh grave of brutal men that couldn't accept when they were beat.

"They dug it themselves," Cara said, staring. "That grave."

"I'd like to think we had some input in digging it for them," Luther said. "After all, it was part of the plan."

"No more cartel," Drake said. "No need to worry about them coming after us." He paused and then said, "Or you."

To his mind, Cara still looked erratic, as if she might try to grab a gun at any minute. "Hey," he said, sitting down next to her. "If there's one thing I know you can do it's make a bloody deal. My advice? Be the first. Your little team here don't sound or look too loyal to me and Jax is going away for years. You don't have to."

"Deal?"

"How many heists have you pulled? Eight? You must know where some of that booty is now, right? The men or women that orchestrated it. The collectors? Do yourself a favor and stay out of jail."

Cara looked grateful. Drake rose and moved away to sit next to Alicia. Her first comment was pretty typical.

"New girlfriend?"

"Backup," Drake said. "In case the current model doesn't pan out. Or gets too old."

She smashed the butt of her gun into his solar plexus.

When Drake could breathe again, he looked at her. "What was that for?"

"Sometimes, Drakey you're a dick."

He looked shocked. Dahl, next to them leaned forward. "She's right, you are."

The Yorkshireman turned to face the Swede. "Piss off, Dahl."

CHAPTER FORTY

A day later and they were back in Las Vegas.

Not at the Azure this time, where they'd recently returned the Fabergé Eggs. They were seated inside Caesar's Palace, close to the entrance to the Forum Shops where the carpeted casino floor gave way to highly polished Italian marble. More specifically, they were seated in a slightly elevated eating area which gave them a panoramic view of the casino floor but was quiet at this time of night as most patrons were either out enjoying the nightlife or gambling.

Drake leaned against a rail that separated the eating area from the rest of the casino. "Not too many aches and pains this time."

"The rest did us good," Hayden said, tackling a thin pair of crepes that had taken over twenty minutes to arrive.

Drake couldn't argue with that but had to comment. "It actually took me a day or so to really hit my stride this time."

Dahl half-choked on his beer. "You hit your stride? Did you get it on video? I never noticed."

Kenzie was looking a little lost. "But what's to come?" she asked. "Next, I mean. I feel . . . homeless. Jobless. Unsure."

"I agree with her," Alicia said. "This break-between-jobs lark is harder than it sounds."

Hayden nodded slowly. "You have to find a hobby."

Alicia cocked her head. "Like what? Badminton?"

"Whatever makes you happy."

"Fighting and killing the scum of the earth makes me

happy. Are you suggesting I confine that to the weekends and one evening, or something?"

"I don't know, Alicia. But give it a chance."

She looked at Drake. "What do you think? I know you agree."

Drake looked to Mai. "I'd like to know what the rest of our team thinks."

The Japanese woman tapped Luther's arm. "We did enjoy our time," she said, "but there's nothing like being back with the team."

Luther grinned. "Yeah, my trigger finger had practically seized up."

One by one, they chimed in. The verdict was unanimous. No more extended layoffs. Hayden broke out her laptop and checked the online HQ. She recorded their status as 'ready' and studied the scrolling feed as it offered jobs. Two were snapped up by others as she watched.

"No shortage of takers," she said. "Looks like everyone feels the same as you guys."

"You can always take a break," Drake said. "Or anyone. We don't all have to be together for every mission."

"There's a job in Iraq. A job in the Amazon basin and another in Australia. Any of those sound good?"

"That's just desert, spiders and heat." Alicia shivered. "No way am I going to any of those places."

"Antarctica?"

"Too cold."

"Right, well where do you want to go?"

Alicia looked up. "Anything in Vegas?"

Drake saved Hayden and asked if there was anything new on the Blood King or the Devil. It turned out a bridge had collapsed two days ago outside New Jersey. Whispers surfacing from the inner workings of the FBI, the CIA and the NSA said all evidence pointed to the work of the Devil. The public at large thought bridge supports had collapsed.

"He's here then," Dahl said. "On American soil."

"All evidence points that way," Hayden said.

There was no sign of the Blood King, not even the faintest whisper. He'd vanished off the face of the earth for now. Of course, one of the main reasons for that was that he might be hiding from the Devil.

Drake looked up as a waitress brought them a fresh round of crepes. They had an assortment of Starbucks coffees, diet Pepsis, sweet and savory pancakes, a Smashburger classic and an Earl of Sandwich gourmet meal. It appeared now that all their food had arrived.

"To Strike Force." Drake raised a cup. "The new SPEAR."

"To Strike Force One," Hayden said. "Best of the elite."

"What exactly are we defined as?" Luther asked.

"Special Operations team," Kinimaka said. "Special Missions unit. A group of people that can come together fast to respond to any and all heavy threats."

"What do you say?" Hayden asked, forking some pancake around her plate. "Shall we meet up again in three weeks?"

"Hawaii," Kinimaka said. "I promised Hay I'd take her back to the homeland. We could all meet up there. It'd be fun."

"Can we kill anyone?" Alicia asked.

"There's always a few bad guys hanging around."

"Good. Then I'm up for it. Not three weeks though."

Mai drank from a bottle of water. "Two? It's hardly worth traveling back to Tokyo for less than two weeks."

"You can come with us," Hayden said quickly. "Honolulu beach will be nice."

Mai shared a wistful glance with Alicia. It was on

Honolulu beach that they'd fought a hard battle against each other in a time that seemed decades past now. But it was slightly less than three years.

"What do you think, Luther?"

"Sure. I never pass up a chance to hit Hawaii."

"To be clear, the only thing we'll be hitting is the beach."

"One week then," Alicia said, glancing around the table. There were nods from Karin, Dino and Molokai. Dahl assured them he'd be there. There was still about a month to go before Johanna moved the kids back to Stockholm.

That left Kenzie and Dallas, who both had another job.

"Whaddya say?" Hayden asked. "Back to task forces, relic smuggling and Egypt or the sun, sand and surf of Oahu?"

"Egypt." Alicia crossed her fingers and closed her eyes, whispering. "Egypt, please Egypt. Choose Egypt."

Kenzie bit her lip. "Well, I guess we're headed to Hawaii then. If Dallas wants to."

The black man nodded. Dahl was watching Kenzie. "Hawaii," he said.

She nodded. Drake was happy. They'd cut their hiatus down from three months to one week. Surely that was long enough for anybody.

He was already itching to get back into the fray. The cartel escape, where he'd been uplifted to see so many soldiers covering his back, had refreshed the old flame. He was ready to save the world again.

"Here's to the next adventure," he said, raising a cup.

A round of cheers met his words. Drake grinned. The future was bright for Strike Force One. Every mission was a gamble with their lives to a degree, he thought, but a gamble loaded in their favor. He drank and took a gander around the casino.

"Speaking of gambling," he said. "Who wants to join me out there?"

He didn't have to check to know they all followed.

THE END

Here ends another Matt Drake story. I hope you enjoyed the new direction that will offer more diverse stories going forward. The two greatest threats will have to be dealt with for sure—the Blood King and the Devil—but there's no rush. I have some entertaining, original adventures planned, both in the standard thriller and archaeological thriller genres. As ever, thanks for all the wonderful, genuine support and, if you'd like to contact me, please do so at the email address below.

Drake 22 will release September/October 2019.

If you enjoyed this book, please leave a review.

Other Books by David Leadbeater:

The Matt Drake Series
A constantly evolving, action-packed romp based in the escapist action-adventure genre:

The Bones of Odin (Matt Drake #1)
The Blood King Conspiracy (Matt Drake #2)
The Gates of Hell (Matt Drake 3)
The Tomb of the Gods (Matt Drake #4)
Brothers in Arms (Matt Drake #5)
The Swords of Babylon (Matt Drake #6)
Blood Vengeance (Matt Drake #7)
Last Man Standing (Matt Drake #8)
The Plagues of Pandora (Matt Drake #9)
The Lost Kingdom (Matt Drake #10)
The Ghost Ships of Arizona (Matt Drake #11)
The Last Bazaar (Matt Drake #12)
The Edge of Armageddon (Matt Drake #13)
The Treasures of Saint Germain (Matt Drake #14)
Inca Kings (Matt Drake #15)
The Four Corners of the Earth (Matt Drake #16)
The Seven Seals of Egypt (Matt Drake #17)
Weapons of the Gods (Matt Drake #18)
The Blood King Legacy (Matt Drake #19)
Devil's Island (Matt Drake #20)

The Alicia Myles Series
Aztec Gold (Alicia Myles #1)
Crusader's Gold (Alicia Myles #2)
Caribbean Gold (Alicia Myles #3)
Chasing Gold (Alecia Myles #4)

The Torsten Dahl Thriller Series
Stand Your Ground (Dahl Thriller #1)

The Relic Hunters Series
The Relic Hunters (Relic Hunters #1)
The Atlantis Cipher (Relic Hunters #2)

The Rogue Series
Rogue (Book One)

The Disavowed Series:
The Razor's Edge (Disavowed #1)
In Harm's Way (Disavowed #2)
Threat Level: Red (Disavowed #3)

The Chosen Few Series
Chosen (The Chosen Trilogy #1)
Guardians (The Chosen Tribology #2)

Short Stories
Walking with Ghosts (A short story)
A Whispering of Ghosts (A short story)

DAVID LEADBEATER

All genuine comments are very welcome at:

davidleadbeater2011@hotmail.co.uk

Twitter: @dleadbeater2011

Visit David's website for the latest news and information:
davidleadbeater.com

Printed in Poland
by Amazon Fulfillment
Poland Sp. z o.o., Wrocław